A HELPING OF HORRID HENRY

Francesca Simon

Illustrated by Tony Ross

Orion
Children's Books

Also by Francesca Simon

CONTENTS

First published in Great Britain in 2001
by Orion Children's Books
a division of the Orion Publishing Group Ltd
Orion House
5 Upper St Martin's Lane
London WC2H 9EA
An Hachette Livre UK Company

22

Text © Francesca Simon *Horrid Henry's Nits* 1997,
Horrid Henry Gets Rich Quick 1998,
Horrid Henry's Haunted House 1999
Illustrations © Tony Ross *Horrid Henry's Nits* 1997,
Horrid Henry Gets Rich Quick 1998,
Horrid Henry's Haunted House 1999

ISBN 978 1 84255 042 7

The Orion Publishing Group's policy is to use papers that
are natural, renewable and recyclable products and
made from wood grown in sustainable forests. The logging
and manufacturing processes are expected to conform to
the environmental regulations of the country of origin.

A catalogue record for this book is available
from the British Library.

Printed in Great Britain by
Clays Ltd, St Ives plc

www.orionbooks.co.uk

HORRID
HENRY'S
NiTS

For my dear friend
Dearbhla Molloy

CONTENTS

1

HORRID HENRY'S NITS

Scratch. Scratch. Scratch.

Dad scratched his head.

"Stop scratching, please," said Mum. "We're eating dinner."

Mum scratched her head.

"Stop scratching, please," said Dad. "We're eating dinner."

Henry scratched his head.

"Stop scratching, Henry!" said Mum and Dad.

"Uh-oh," said Mum. She put down her fork and frowned at Henry.

"Henry, do you have nits *again*?"

"Of course not," said Henry.

"Come over to the sink, Henry," said Mum.

"Why?" said Henry.

"I need to check your head."

Henry dragged his feet over to her as slowly as possible. It's not fair, he thought. It wasn't his fault nits loved him. Henry's head was a gathering place for nits far and wide. They probably held nit parties there and foreign nits visited him on their holidays.

Mum dragged the nit comb across Henry's head. She made a face and groaned.

"You're crawling with nits, Henry," said Mum.

"Ooh, let's see," said Henry. He always liked counting how many nits he had.

"One, two, three . . . forty-five, forty-six, forty-seven . . ." he counted, dropping them on to a paper towel.

"It's not polite to count nits," said his younger brother, Perfect Peter, wiping his mouth with his spotless napkin, "is it, Mum?"

"It certainly isn't," said Mum.

Dad dragged the nit comb across his head and made a face.

"Ughh," said Dad.

Mum dragged the comb through

her hair.

"Bleeeech," said Mum.

Mum combed Perfect Peter's hair. Then she did it again. And again. And again.

"No nits, Peter," said Mum, smiling. "As usual. Well done, darling."

Perfect Peter smiled modestly.

"It's because I wash and comb my hair every night," said Peter.

Henry scowled. True, his hair was filthy, but then . . .

"Nits love clean hair," said Henry.

"No they don't," said Peter. "*I've* never ever had nits."

We'll see about that, thought Henry. When no one was looking he picked a few nits off the paper towel. Then he wandered over to Peter and casually fingered a lock of his hair.

LEAP!

Scratch. Scratch.

"Mum!" squealed Peter. "Henry's pulling my hair!"

"Stop it, Henry," said Dad.

"I wasn't pulling his hair," said Henry indignantly. "I just wanted to see how clean it was. And it is so lovely and clean," added Henry sweetly. "I wish my hair was as clean as Peter's."

Peter beamed. It wasn't often that Henry said anything nice to him.

"Right," said Mum grimly, "everyone upstairs. It's shampoo time."

"NO!" shrieked Horrid Henry. "NO SHAMPOO!"

He hated the stinky smelly horrible shampoo much more than he hated having nits. Only today his teacher,

Miss Battle-Axe, had sent home a nit letter.

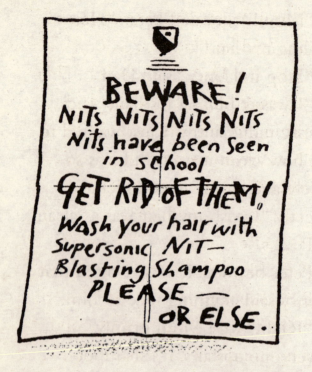

BEWARE!
NiTs NiTs NiTs NiTs
NiTs have been seen
in school
GET RID OF THEM!
Wash your hair with
Supersonic NiT—
Blasting Shampoo
PLEASE —
OR ELSE..

Naturally, Henry had crumpled up the letter and thrown it away. He was never ever going to have pongy nit shampoo on his head again. What rotten luck Mum had spotted him scratching.

"It's the only way to get rid of nits," said Dad.

"But it never works!" screamed Henry. And he ran for the door.

Mum and Dad grabbed him. Then they dragged him kicking and screaming to the bathroom.

"Nits are living creatures," howled Henry. "Why kill them?"

"Because . . ." said Mum.

"Because . . . because . . . they're blood-sucking nits," said Dad.

Blood-sucking. Henry had never thought of that. In the split second that he stood still to consider this interesting information, Mum emptied the bottle of supersonic nit-blasting shampoo over his hair.

"NO!" screamed Henry. Frantically he shook his head. There was shampoo on the door. There was shampoo on the floor. There was shampoo all over Mum and Dad. The only place there was no shampoo was on Henry's head.

"Henry! Stop being horrid!" yelled Dad, wiping shampoo off his shirt.

"What a big fuss over nothing," said Peter.

Henry lunged at him. Mum seized Henry by the collar and held him back.

"Now Peter," said Mum. "That wasn't a kind thing to say to Henry, was it? Not everyone is as brave as you."

"You're right, Mum," said Perfect Peter. "I was being rude and thoughtless. It won't happen again. I'm so sorry, Henry."

Mum smiled at him. "That was a perfect apology, Peter. As for you, Henry . . ." she sighed. "We'll get more shampoo tomorrow."

Phew, thought Henry, giving his head an extra good scratch. Safe for one more day.

The next morning at school a group of parents burst into the classroom, waving the nit letter and shouting.

"My Margaret doesn't have nits!" shrieked Moody Margaret's mother.

"She never has and she never will. How dare you send home such a letter!"

"My Josh doesn't have nits," shouted his mother. "The idea!"

"My Toby doesn't have nits!" shouted his father. "Some nasty child in this class isn't bug-busting!"

Miss Battle-Axe squared her shoulders.

"Rest assured that the culprit will be found," she said. "I have declared war on nits."

Scratch. Scratch. Scratch.

Miss Battle-Axe spun round. Her beady eyes swivelled over the class.

"Who's scratching?" she demanded.

Silence.

Henry bent over his worksheet and tried to look studious.

"Henry is," said Moody Margaret.

"Liar!" shouted Horrid Henry. "It was William!"

Weepy William burst into tears.

"No it wasn't," he sobbed.

Miss Battle-Axe glared at the class.

"I'm going to find out once and for all who's got nits," she growled.

"I don't!" shouted Moody Margaret.

"I don't!" shouted Rude Ralph.

"I don't!" shouted Horrid Henry.

"Silence!" ordered Miss Battle-Axe. "Nora, the nit nurse, is coming this morning. Who's got nits? Who's not bug-busting? We'll all find out soon."

Uh-oh, thought Henry. Now I'm sunk. There was no escaping Nitty Nora Bug Explorer and her ferocious combs. Everyone would know *he* had the nits. Rude Ralph would never stop teasing him. He'd be shampooed every night. Mum and Dad would find out about all the nit letters he'd thrown away . . .

He could of course get a tummy ache double quick and be sent home. But Nitty Nora had a horrible way of remembering whose head she hadn't checked and then combing it in front of the whole class.

He could run screaming out of the door saying he'd caught mad cow disease. But somehow he didn't think Miss Battle-Axe would believe him.

There was no way out. This time he was well and truly stuck.

Unless . . .

Suddenly Henry had a wonderful, spectacular idea. It was so wicked, and so horrible, that even Horrid Henry hesitated. But only for a moment. Desperate times call for desperate measures.

Henry leaned over Clever Clare and brushed his head lightly against hers.

LEAP!

Scratch. Scratch.

"Get away from me, Henry," hissed Clare.

"I was just admiring your lovely picture," said Henry.

He got up to sharpen his pencil. On his way to the sharpener he brushed against Greedy Graham.

LEAP!

Scratch. Scratch.

On his way back from the sharpener Henry stumbled and fell against Anxious Andrew.

LEAP!

Scratch. Scratch.

"Ow!" yelped Andrew.

"Sorry, Andrew," said Henry.
"What big clumsy feet I have.
Whoops!" he added, tripping over the
carpet and banging heads with Weepy
William.

LEAP!

Scratch. Scratch.

"Waaaaaaaaa!" wailed William.

"Sit down at once, Henry," said
Miss Battle-Axe. "William! Stop
scratching. Bert! How do you spell
cat?"

"I dunno," said Beefy Bert.

Horrid Henry leaned across the
table and put his head close to Bert's.

"C-A-T," he whispered helpfully.

LEAP!

Scratch. Scratch.

Then Horrid Henry raised his hand.

"Yes?" said Miss Battle-Axe.

"I don't understand these

instructions," said Henry sweetly.
"Could you help me, please?"

Miss Battle-Axe frowned. She
liked to keep as far away from Henry
as possible. Reluctantly she came
closer and bent over his work. Henry
leaned his head near hers.

LEAP!

Scratch. Scratch.

There was a pounding at the door.
Then Nitty Nora marched into the
classroom, bristling with combs and
other instruments of torture.

"Line up, everyone,"
said Miss Battle-Axe,
patting her hair. "The
nit nurse is here."

Rats, thought Henry. He'd hardly started. Slowly he stood up.

Everyone pushed and shoved to be first in line. Then a few children remembered what they were lining up for and stampeded towards the back. Horrid Henry saw his chance and took it.

He charged through the squabbling children, brushing against everyone as fast as he could.

LEAP!

Scratch! Scratch!

LEAP!

Scratch! Scratch!

LEAP!

Scratch! Scratch!

"Henry!" shouted Miss Battle-Axe. "Stay in at playtime. Now go to the end of the queue. The rest of you, stop this nonsense at once!"

Moody Margaret had fought longest and hardest to be first. Proudly she presented her head to Nitty Nora.

"I certainly don't have nits," she said.

Nitty Nora stuck the comb in.

"Nits!" she announced, stuffing a nit note into Margaret's hand.

For once Margaret was too shocked to speak.

"But . . . but . . ." she gasped.

Tee-hee, thought Henry. Now he wouldn't be the only one.

"Next," said Nitty Nora.

She stuck the comb in Rude Ralph's greasy hair.

"Nits!" she announced.

"Nit-face," hissed Horrid Henry, beside himself with glee.

"Nits!" said Nitty Nora, poking her comb into Lazy Linda's mop.

"Nits!" said Nitty Nora, prodding Greedy Graham's frizzy hair.

"Nits, nits, nits, nits, nits!" she continued, pointing at Weepy William, Clever Clare, Sour Susan, Beefy Bert and Dizzy Dave.

Then Nitty Nora beckoned to Miss Battle-Axe.

"Teachers too," she ordered.

Miss Battle-Axe's jaw dropped.

"I have been teaching for twenty-five years and I have never had nits," she said. "Don't waste your time checking *me*."

Nitty Nora ignored her protests and stuck in the comb.

"Hmmn," she said, and whispered in Miss Battle-Axe's ear.

"NO!" howled Miss Battle-Axe.

"NOOOOOOOOOO!" Then she joined the line of weeping, wailing children clutching their nit notes.

At last it was Henry's turn.

Nitty Nora stuck her comb into Henry's tangled hair and dragged it along his scalp. She combed again. And again. And again.

"No nits," said Nitty Nora. "Keep up the good work, young man."

"I sure will!" said Henry.

Horrid Henry skipped home waving his certificate.

"Look, Peter," crowed Henry. "I'm nit-free!"

Perfect Peter burst into tears.

"I'm not," he wailed.

"Hard luck," said Horrid Henry.

2

HORRID HENRY AND THE FANGMANGLER

Horrid Henry snatched his skeleton bank and tried to twist open the trap door. Mum was taking him to Toy Heaven tomorrow. At last Henry would be able to buy the toy of his dreams: a Dungeon Drink kit. Ha ha ha – the tricks he'd play on his family, substituting their drinks for Dungeon stinkers.

Best of all, Moody Margaret would be green with envy. She wanted a

Dungeon Drink kit too, but she
didn't have any money. He'd have
one first, and no way was Margaret
ever going to play with it. Except for
buying the occasional sweet and a few
comics, Henry had been saving his
money for weeks.

Perfect Peter peeked round the
door.

"I've saved £7.53," said Peter
proudly, jingling his piggy bank.
"More than enough to buy my nature
kit. How much do you have?"

"Millions," said Henry.

Perfect Peter gasped.

"You do not," said Peter. "Do
you?"

Henry shook his bank. A thin rattle
came from within.

"That doesn't sound like millions,"
said Peter.

"That's 'cause five pound notes
don't rattle, stupid," said Henry.

"Mum! Henry called me stupid,"
shrieked Peter.

"Stop being horrid, Henry!"
shouted Mum.

Horrid Henry gave the lid of his
bank a final yank and spilled the
contents on to the floor.

A single, solitary five pence coin
rolled out.

Henry's jaw dropped. He grabbed the bank and fumbled around inside. It was empty.

"I've been robbed!" howled Horrid Henry. "Where's my money? Who stole my money?"

Mum ran into the room.

"What's all this fuss?"

"Peter stole my money!" screamed Henry. He glared at his brother. "Just wait until I get my hands on you, you little thief, I'll —"

"No one stole your money, Henry," said Mum. "You've spent it all on sweets and comics."

"I have not!" shrieked Henry.

Mum pointed at the enormous pile of comics and sweet wrappers littering the floor of Henry's bedroom.

"What's all that then?" asked Mum.

Horrid Henry stopped shrieking. It was true. He *had* spent all his pocket money on comics and sweets. He just hadn't noticed.

"It's not fair!" he screamed.

"I saved all0 pocket money, Mum," said Perfect Peter. "After all, a penny saved is a penny earned."

Mum smiled at him. "Well done, Peter. Henry, let this be a lesson to you."

"I can't wait to buy my nature kit,"
said Perfect Peter. "You should have
saved your money like I did, instead of
wasting it, Henry."

Henry growled and sprang at Peter.
He was an Indian warrior scalping
a settler.

"YOWWWW!" squealed Peter.

"Henry! Stop it!" shouted Mum.
"Say sorry to Peter."

"I'm not sorry!" screamed Henry.
"I want my money!"

"Any more nonsense from you, young man, and we won't be going to Toy Heaven," said Mum.

Henry scowled.

"I don't care," he muttered. What was the point of going to Toy Heaven if he couldn't buy any toys?

Horrid Henry lay on his bedroom
floor kicking sweet wrappers. That
Dungeon Drink kit cost £4.99. He had
to get some money by tomorrow.
The question was, how?

He could steal Peter's money. That
was tempting, as he knew the secret
place in Peter's cello case where Peter
hid his bank. Wouldn't that be fun
when Peter discovered his money was
gone? Henry smiled.

On second thought, perhaps not.
Mum and Dad would be sure to
suspect Henry, especially if he
suddenly had money and Peter didn't.

He could sell some of his comics to
Moody Margaret.

"No!" shrieked Henry, clutching
his comics to his chest. Not his
precious comics. There *had* to be
another way.

Then Henry had a wonderful, spectacular idea. It was so superb that he did a wild war dance for joy. That Dungeon Drink kit was as good as his. And, better still, Peter would give him all the money he needed. Henry chortled. This would be as easy as taking sweets from a baby . . . and a lot more fun.

Horrid Henry strolled down the hall to Peter's room. Peter was having a meeting of the Best Boys Club (motto: Can I help?) with his friends Tidy Ted, Spotless Sam and Goody-Goody Gordon. What luck. More money for him. Henry smiled as he put his ear to the keyhole and listened to them discussing their good deeds.

"I helped an old lady cross the road

and I ate all my vegetables," said
Perfect Peter.

"I kept my room tidy all week,"
said Tidy Ted.

"I scrubbed the bath without being
asked," said Spotless Sam.

"I never once forgot to say please
and thank you," said Goody-Goody
Gordon.

Henry pushed past the barricades
and burst into Peter's room.

"Password!" screeched Perfect
Peter.

"Vitamins," said Horrid Henry.

"How did you know?" said Tidy
Ted, staring open-mouthed at Henry.

"Never you mind," said Henry,
who was not a master spy for
nothing. "I don't suppose any of you
know about Fangmanglers?"

The boys looked at one another.

"What are they?" asked Spotless Sam.

"Only the slimiest, scariest, most horrible and frightening monsters in the whole world," said Henry. "And I know where to find one."

"Where?" said Goody-Goody Gordon.

"I'm not going to tell you," said Horrid Henry.

"Oh please!" said Spotless Sam.

Henry shook his head and lowered his voice.

"Fangmanglers only come out at night," whispered Henry. "They slip into the shadows then sneak out and . . . BITE YOU!" he suddenly shrieked.

The Best Boys Club members gasped with fright.

"I'm not scared," said Peter. "And I've never heard of a Fangmangler."

"That's because you're too young," said Henry. "Grown-ups don't tell you about them because they don't want to scare you."

"I want to see it," said Tidy Ted.

"Me too," said Spotless Sam and Goody-Goody Gordon.

Peter hesitated for a moment.

"Is this a trick, Henry?"

"Of course not," said Henry. "And just for that I won't let you come."

"Oh please, Henry," said Peter.

Henry paused.

"All right," he said. "We'll meet in the back garden after dark. But it will cost you two pounds each."

"Two pounds!" they squealed.

"Do you want to see a Fangmangler or don't you?"

Perfect Peter exchanged a look with his friends.

They all nodded.

"Good," said Horrid Henry. "See you at six o'clock. And don't forget to bring your money."

Tee hee, chortled Henry silently.

Eight pounds! He could get a
Dungeon Drink kit *and* a Grisly
Ghoul Grub box at this rate.

Loud screams came from next-
door's garden.

"Give me back my spade!" came
Moody Margaret's bossy tones.

"You're so mean, Margaret,"
squealed Sour Susan's sulky voice.
"Well, I won't. It's my turn to dig
with it now."

WHACK! THWACK!

"WAAAAAAA!"

Eight pounds is nice, thought
Horrid Henry, but twelve is even
nicer.

"What's going on?" asked Horrid
Henry, smirking as he leapt over the
wall.

"Go away, Henry!" shouted
Moody Margaret.

"Yeah, Henry," echoed Sour Susan, wiping away her tears. "We don't want you."

"All right," said Henry. "Then I won't tell you about the Fangmangler I've found."

"We don't want to know about it," said Margaret, turning her back on him.

"That's right," said Susan.

"Well then, don't blame me when the Fangmangler sneaks over the wall and rips you to pieces and chews up your guts," said Horrid Henry. He turned to go.

The girls looked at one another.

"Wait," ordered Margaret.

"Yeah?" said Henry.

"You don't scare me," said Margaret.

"Prove it then," said Henry.

"How?" said Margaret.

"Be in my garden at six o'clock tonight and I'll show you the Fangmangler. But it will cost you two pounds each."

"Forget it," said Margaret. "Come on, Susan."

"Okay," said Henry quickly. "One pound each."

"No," said Margaret.

"And your money back if the Fangmangler doesn't scare you," said Henry.

Moody Margaret smiled.

"It's a deal," she said.

When the coast was clear, Horrid Henry crept into the bushes and hid a bag containing his supplies: an old, torn T-shirt, some filthy trousers and

a jumbo-sized bottle of ketchup.
Then he sneaked back into the house
and waited for dark.

"Thank you, thank you, thank you,
thank you," said Horrid Henry,
collecting two pounds from each
member of the Best Boys Club.
Henry placed the money carefully in
his skeleton bank. Boy, was he rich!

Moody Margaret and Sour Susan
handed over one pound each.

"Remember Henry, we get our
money back if we aren't scared,"
hissed Moody Margaret.

"Shut up, Margaret," said Henry.
"I'm risking my life and all you can
think about is money. Now
everyone, wait here, don't move and
don't talk," he whispered. "We have
to surprise the Fangmangler. If

not . . ." Henry paused and drew his fingers across his throat. "I'm a goner. I'm going off now to hunt for the monster. When I find him, and if it's safe, I'll whistle twice. Then everyone come, as quietly as you can. But be careful!"

Henry disappeared into the black darkness of the garden.

For a long long moment there was silence.

"This is stupid," said Moody Margaret.

Suddenly, a low, moaning growl echoed through the moonless night.

"What was that?" said Spotless Sam nervously.

"Henry? Are you all right, Henry?" squeaked Perfect Peter.

The low moaning growl turned into a snarl.

THRASH! CRASH!

"HELP! HELP! THE FANGMANGLER'S AFTER ME! RUN FOR YOUR LIVES!" screamed Horrid Henry, smashing through the bushes. His T-shirt and trousers were torn. There was blood everywhere.

The Best Boys Club screamed and ran.

Sour Susan screamed and ran.

Moody Margaret screamed and ran.

Horrid Henry screamed and . . . stopped.

He waited until he was alone. Then

Horrid Henry wiped some ketchup from his face, clutched his bank and did a war dance round the garden, whooping with joy.

"Money! Money! Money! Money! Money!" he squealed, leaping and stomping. He danced and he pranced, he twirled and he whirled. He was so busy dancing and cackling he didn't notice a shadowy shape slip into the garden behind him.

"Money! Money! Money! Mine! Mine —" he broke off. What was that noise? Horrid Henry's throat tightened.

"Nah," he thought. "It's nothing."

Then suddenly a dark shape leapt out of the bushes and let out a thunderous roar.

Horrid Henry shrieked with terror. He dropped his money and ran for his life. The Thing scooped up his bank and slithered over the wall.

Horrid Henry did not stop running until he was safely in his room with the door shut tight and barricaded. His heart pounded.

There really is a Fangmangler, he thought, trembling. And now it's after *me*.

Horrid Henry hardly slept a wink. He started awake at every squeak and creak. He shook and he shrieked. Henry had such a bad night that he slept in quite late the next morning, tossing and turning.

FIZZ! POP! GURGLE! BANG!

Henry jerked awake. What was that? He peeked his head out from under the duvet and listened.

FIZZ! POP! GURGLE! BANG!

Those fizzing and popping noises seemed to be coming from next door.

Henry ran to the window and pulled open the curtains. There was Moody Margaret sitting beside a large Toy Heaven bag. In front of her was . . . a Dungeon Drink kit. She saw him, smiled, and raised a glass of bubbling black liquid.

"Want a Fangmangler drink, Henry?" asked Margaret sweetly.

3

HORRID HENRY'S SCHOOL TRIP

"Don't forget my packed lunch for the school trip," shouted Horrid Henry for the tenth time. "I want crisps, biscuits, chocolate, and a fizzywizz drink."

"No way, Henry," said Dad grimly, slicing carrots. "I'm making you a healthy, nutritious lunch."

"But I don't want a healthy lunch," howled Henry. "I like sweets!"

"Sweets, yuck," said Perfect Peter.

He peeked in his lunch box.

"Oh boy, an apple!" said Peter. "And egg and cress on brown bread with the crusts on! And carrot and celery sticks, my favourite! Thank you so much, Dad. Henry, if you don't eat healthy food, you'll never grow big and strong."

"Oh yeah," said Henry. "I'll show you how big and strong I am, you little pipsqueak," he added, springing at Peter. He was a boa constrictor throttling his prey.

"Uggghhhh," choked Peter.

"Stop being horrid, Henry!" shouted Mum. "Or there will be no school trip for you."

Henry let Peter go. Horrid Henry loved school trips. No work. No assembly. A packed lunch. A chance to fool around all day. What could be better?

"I'm going to the Frosty Freeze Ice Cream factory," said Henry. "Free ice creams for everyone. Yippee!"

Perfect Peter made a face. "I don't like ice cream," he said. "My class is going somewhere much better – our Town Museum. And Mum's coming to help."

"I'd rather be boiled alive and eaten by cannibals than go to that boring old dump," said Horrid Henry, shuddering. Mum had dragged him there once. Never again.

Then Henry noticed Peter's T-shirt. It was exactly the same as his, purple striped with gold stars.

"Tell Peter to stop copying what I wear to school!" screamed Henry.

"It doesn't matter, Henry," said Mum. "You're going on different trips. No one will notice."

"Just keep out of my way, Peter," snarled Henry. "I don't want anyone to think we're related."

Horrid Henry's class buzzed with excitement as they scrambled to be first on the bus.

"I've got crisps!" shouted Dizzy Dave.

"I've got biscuits!" shouted Anxious Andrew.

"I've got toffee and chocolate and lollies and three fizzywizzes!" shouted Greedy Graham.

"WAAAA," wailed Weepy
William. "I forgot my packed lunch."

"Quiet!" ordered Miss Battle-Axe
as the bus started moving. "Sit still
and behave. No eating on the bus.
William, stop weeping."

"I need a wee!" shouted Lazy Linda.

"Well, you'll have to wait,"
snapped Miss Battle-Axe.

Horrid Henry had trampled his
way to the window seats at the back
next to Rude Ralph and Greedy
Graham. He liked those seats best.
Miss Battle-Axe couldn't see him, and
he could make faces at all the people
in the cars behind him.

Henry and Ralph rolled down the
window and chanted:

"Beans, beans, good for the heart,
The more you eat, the more you –"

"HENRY!" bellowed Miss

Battle-Axe. "Turn around and face forward NOW!"

"I need a wee!" shouted Dizzy Dave.

"Look what I've got, Henry," said Greedy Graham, holding a bulging bag of sweets.

"Gimme some," said Henry.

"And me," said Rude Ralph.

The three boys stuffed their faces with sweets.

"Ugh, a green lime," said Henry, taking the sticky sweet out of his mouth. "Eeech." He flicked the sweet away.

PING!

The sweet landed on Moody Margaret's neck.

"Ow," said Margaret.

She turned round and glared at Henry.

"Stop it, Henry!" she snarled.

"I didn't do anything," said Henry.

PING!

A sweet landed in Sour Susan's hair.

PING!

A sweet stuck on Anxious Andrew's new jumper.

"Henry's throwing sweets!" shouted Margaret.

Miss Battle-Axe turned round.

"Henry! Sit next to me," she said.

"I need a wee!" wailed Weepy William.

Finally, the bus drove up to the
Frosty Freeze Factory. A gigantic,
delicious-looking ice cream cone
loomed above it.

"We're here!" shouted Henry.

"You scream! I scream! We all
scream for ice cream!" shrieked the
children as the bus stopped outside
the gate.

"Why are we waiting here?" yelled
Greedy Graham. "I want my ice
creams now!"

Henry stuck his head out of the
window. The gates were chained
shut. A large sign read: "CLOSED
on Mondays."

Miss Battle-Axe looked pale. "I
don't believe this," she muttered.

"Class, there's been a mix-up, and
we seem to have come on the wrong
day," said Miss Battle-Axe. "But

never mind. We'll go to –"

"The Science Museum!" shouted Clever Clare.

"The zoo!" shouted Dizzy Dave.

"Lazer Zap!" shouted Horrid Henry.

"No," said Miss Battle-Axe. "Our Town Museum."

"Ugggghhhhh," groaned the class.

No one groaned louder than Horrid Henry.

The children left their jackets and lunch boxes in the packed lunch room, and then followed the museum guide to Room 1.

"First we'll see Mr Jones's collection of rubber bands," said the guide. "Then our famous display of door hinges and dog collars through history. And don't worry, you'll be seeing our latest acquisitions, soil from Miss Montague's garden and the Mayor's baby pictures."

Horrid Henry had to escape.

"I need a wee," said Henry.

"Hurry up then," said Miss Battle-Axe. "And come straight back."

The toilets were next to the packed lunch room.

Henry thought he'd make sure his lunch was still there. Yup, there it was, right next to Ralph's.

I wonder what Ralph has got, thought Henry, staring at Ralph's packed lunch. No harm in looking.

WOW. Rude Ralph's lunch box was bursting with crisps, sweets, and a chocolate spread sandwich on white bread.

He'll feel sick if he eats all that junk

food, thought Henry. I'd better help
him.

It was the work of a moment to
swap Ralph's sandwich for Henry's
egg and cress.

This certainly isn't very healthy,
thought Henry, gazing at Greedy
Graham's goodies. I'll do him a
favour and exchange a few of my
celery sticks for his sweets.

Just look at all those treats, thought
Henry, fingering Sour Susan's cakes.
She should eat a more balanced meal.

A pack of raisins zipped from
Henry's lunch box to Susan's and a
sticky bun leapt from Susan's to
Henry's.

Tsk tsk, thought Henry, helping
himself to Tough Toby's chocolate
bar and replacing it with an apple.
Too many sweets are bad for the
teeth.

That's better, he thought, gazing at his re-packed lunch with satisfaction. Then he strolled back to his class, who were gathered round a glass case.

"This is the soil in which Miss Montague grew her prize-winning vegetables," droned the guide. "She grew marrows, tomatoes, potatoes, leeks –"

"When do we eat?" interrupted Horrid Henry.

"I'm starving," whined Greedy Graham.

"My tummy's rumbling," groaned Rude Ralph.

"When's lunch?" moaned Moody Margaret.

"WE'RE HUNGRY!" wailed the children.

"All right," said Miss Battle-Axe. "We'll eat now."

The class stampeded down the hall and grabbed their lunches. Henry sat in a corner and tucked in.

For a moment there was silence, then the room echoed with howls of dismay.

"Where's my sticky bun?" yelped Sour Susan.

"My sweets are gone!" screamed Greedy Graham.

"What's this? Egg and cress? Yuck!" shouted Rude Ralph, hurling the sandwich at Anxious Andrew.

That did it. The room filled with flying carrot and celery sticks, granola bars, raisins, crusts, and apples. Henry smirked as he wiped the last traces of chocolate from his mouth.

"Stop it! Stop it!" howled Miss Battle-Axe. "Well done, Henry, for being the only sensible child. You may lead us back to see the pieces of Roman pottery in Room 2."

Horrid Henry walked proudly at the head of the shuffling, whining children. Then he noticed the lift at the far end. A sign read:

STAFF ONLY:

DO NOT ENTER

I wonder where that lift goes, thought Horrid Henry.

"Stop him!" yelled a guard.

But it was too late.

Henry had dashed to the lift and pressed the top button.

Up up up he zipped.

Henry found himself in a small room filled with half-finished exhibits. On display were lists of

overdue library books, "lightbulbs
from 1965 to today," and rows and
rows of rocks.

Then, in the corner, Henry actually
saw something interesting: a dog's
skeleton protected by a drooping blue
cord.

Henry looked more closely.

It's just a pile of bones, thought
Henry.

He wobbled the blue cord then
stood on it.

"Look at me, I'm a tight-rope walker," chortled Horrid Henry, swaying on the blue cord. "I'm the best tight-rope walker in – AGGGHHHH!"

Horrid Henry lost his balance and toppled against the skeleton.

CLITTER-CLATTER! The bones crashed to the ground.

DING DING DING. A burglar alarm began to wail.

Museum guards ran into the room.

Uh-oh, thought Horrid Henry. He slipped between a guard's legs and ran. Behind him he could hear pounding feet.

Henry dashed into a large room filled with road signs, used bus tickets and traffic cones. At the other end of the room Henry saw Peter's class gathered in front of "The Story of the drain". Oh no. There was Mum.

Henry ducked behind the traffic cones.

Museum guards entered.

"There he is!" shouted one. "The boy in the purple T-shirt with the gold stars."

Henry stood fixed to the spot. He was trapped. Then the guards ran straight past his hiding place. A long arm reached over and plucked Perfect Peter from his group.

"Come with us, you!" snarled the guard. "We're going straight to the Bad Children's Room."

"But . . . but . . ." gasped Peter.

"No ifs or buts!" snapped the guard. "Who's in charge of this child?"

"I am," said Mum. "What's the meaning of this?"

"You come too," ordered the guard.

"But . . . but . . ." gasped Mum.

Shouting and protesting, Mum and Perfect Peter were taken away.

Then Henry heard a familiar booming voice.

"Margaret, that's enough pushing," said Miss Battle-Axe. "No touching, Ralph. Stop weeping, William. Hurry up, everyone! The bus leaves in five minutes. Walk quietly to the exit."

Everyone immediately started running.

Horrid Henry waited until most of the children had charged past then re-joined the group.

"Where have you been, Henry?" snapped Miss Battle-Axe.

"Just enjoying this brilliant museum," said Horrid Henry. "When can we come back?"

4

HORRID HENRY AND THE DINNER GUESTS

FIZZ! POP! GURGLE! BANG!

Horrid Henry sat on the kitchen floor watching his new Dungeon Drink kit brew a bubbly purple potion.

BELCH! CRUNCH! OOZE! SPLAT!

Beside it, a Grisly Ghoul Grub box heaved and spewed some Rotten Crispies.

Dad dashed into the kitchen.

"Want a crisp?" said Henry, smirking.

"No!" said Dad, putting on his apron. "And I've told you before to play with those disgusting kits in your bedroom."

Why Henry's grandmother had bought him those terrible toys for Christmas he would never know.

"Henry, I want you to listen carefully," said Dad, feverishly rolling out pastry. "Mum's new boss and her husband are coming to dinner in an hour. I want total cooperation and perfect behaviour."

"Yeah, yeah," said Henry, his eyes glued to the frothing machine.

Horrid Henry's parents didn't have guests for dinner very often. The last time they did Henry had sneaked downstairs, eaten the entire chocolate

cake Dad had baked for dessert and
then been sick all over the sofa. The
time before that he'd put whoopee
cushions on all the guests' seats,
bitten Peter, and broken the banister
by sliding down it.

PRRRRRP

Dad started getting pots and pans
down.

"What are you cooking?" said
Perfect Peter, tidying up his stamps.

79

"Salmon wrapped in pastry with lime and ginger," said Dad, staring at his list.

"Yummy!" said Perfect Peter. "My favourite!"

"Yuck!" said Horrid Henry. "I want pizza. What's for pudding?"

"Chocolate mousse," said Dad.

"Can I help?" said Peter.

"Of course," said Mum, smiling. "You can pass round the nuts and crisps when Mr and Mrs Mossy arrive."

Nuts? Crisps? Henry's ears perked up.

"I'll help too," said Henry.

Mum looked at him. "We'll see," she said.

"I don't think Henry should pass round the nuts," said Peter. "He'll only eat them himself."

"Shut up, Peter," snarled Henry.

"Mum! Henry told me to shut up!" wailed Peter.

"Henry! Stop being horrid," muttered Dad, grating ginger and squeezing limes.

While Dad rolled up salmon in pastry, Mum dashed about setting the table with the best china.

"Hey! You haven't set enough places," said Henry. "You've only set the table for four."

"That's right," said Mum. "Mrs Mossy, Mr Mossy, Dad and me."

"What about me?" said Henry.

"And me?" said Peter.

"This is a grown-ups' party," said Mum.

"You want me . . . to go . . . to bed?" Henry stuttered. "I'm not . . . eating with you?"

"No," said Dad.

"It's not fair!" shrieked Henry.
"What am I having for supper then?"

"A cheese sandwich," said Dad.
"We've got to get ready for the guests.
I'm already two minutes behind my
schedule."

"I'm not eating this swill!"
shrieked Henry, shoving the
sandwich off his plate. "I want pizza!"

"That's all right, Dad," said Peter,
tucking into his sandwich. "I
understand that grown-ups need to be
by themselves sometimes."

Henry lunged at Peter. He was a
cannibal trussing his victim for the
pot.

"AAARGHH!" shrieked Peter.

"That's it, Henry, go to bed!"
shouted Mum.

"I won't!" screamed Henry. "I
want chocolate mousse!"

"Go upstairs and stay upstairs!" shouted Mum.

Ding dong!

"Aaagh!" squealed Dad. "They're early! I haven't finished the mousse yet."

Horrid Henry stomped upstairs to his bedroom and slammed the door.

He was so angry he could hardly speak. The injustice of it all. Why should he go to bed while Mum and Dad were downstairs having fun and eating chocolate mousse? The delicious smell of melting chocolate wafted into his nostrils. Henry's tummy rumbled. If Mum and Dad thought he'd stay in bed while they all had fun downstairs they had rocks for brains.

SCREEEECH! SCREEEECH!

Perfect Peter must be playing his cello for Mum and Dad and the guests. Which meant . . . Horrid Henry smiled. The coast was clear. Hello, nuts, here I come, thought Henry.

Henry tip-toed downstairs. The screechy-scratchy sounds continued from the sitting room.

Horrid Henry sneaked into the empty kitchen. There were the bowls of nuts and crisps and the drinks all ready to serve.

Cashews, my favourite. I'll just have a few, he thought.

Chomp. Chomp. Chomp.

Hmmn, boy, those nuts were good. Irresistible, really, thought Henry. A few more would go down a treat. And, if he poured the remaining nuts into a smaller bowl, no one would notice how many he'd eaten.

CHOMP! CHOMP! CHOMP!

Just one more, thought Henry, and that's it.

Horrid Henry swizzled his fingers round the nut bowl.

Uh-oh. There were only three nuts left.

Yikes, thought Henry. Now I'm in trouble.

FIZZ! POP! GURGLE! BANG!
BELCH! CRUNCH! OOZE!
SPLAT!

Horrid Henry looked at his Grisly
Grub box and Dungeon Drink kit
and bopped himself on the head.
What an idiot he was. What better
time to try out his grisly grub than
. . . now?

Henry examined the Rotten
Crispies he'd made earlier. They
looked like crisps, but certainly didn't
taste like them. The only problem
was, what to do with the good crisps?

Yum yum! thought Henry,
crunching crisps as fast as he could.
Then he re-filled the bowl with
Rotten Crispies.

Next, Henry poured two frothing
dungeon drinks into glasses, and put
them on the tray.

Perfect, thought Henry. Now to make some Nasty Nuts to replace all those cashews.

The kitchen door opened. Dad came in.

"What are you doing, Henry? I told you to go to bed."

"Mum said I could serve the nuts," said Henry, lying shamelessly. Then he grabbed the two bowls and escaped.

The sound of applause came from the sitting room. Perfect Peter bowed modestly.

"Isn't he adorable?" said Mrs Mossy.

"And so talented," said Mr Mossy.

"Hello, Mr and Mrs Bossy," said Henry.

Mum looked horrified.

"Mossy, not Bossy, dear" said Mum.

"But that's what you call them, Mum," said Henry, smiling sweetly.

"Henry is just going to bed," said Mum, blushing.

"No I wasn't," said Henry. "I was going to serve the nuts and crisps. Don't you remember?"

"Oooh, I love nuts," said Mrs Mossy.

"I told you to stay upstairs," hissed Mum.

"Muuuum," wailed Peter. "You said I could serve the guests."

"You can serve the crisps, Peter," said Henry graciously, handing him the bowl of Rotten Crispies. "Would you like a cashew, Mrs Bossy?"

"Mossy!" hissed Mum.

"Ooh, cashews, my favourite," said Mrs Mossy. She plunged her fingers into the mostly empty nut bowl, and finally scooped up the remaining three.

Henry snatched two back.

"You're only supposed to have one nut at a time," he said. "Don't be greedy."

"Henry!" said Mum. "Don't be rude."

"Want a nut?" said Henry, waving

the bowl in front of Mr Mossy.

"Why, yes, I . . ." said Mr Mossy.

But he was too late. Henry had already moved away to serve Mum.

"Want a nut?" he asked.

Mum's hand reached out to take one, but Henry quickly whisked the bowl away.

"Henry!" said Mum.

"Do have some crisps, Mrs Mossy," said Perfect Peter. Mrs Mossy scooped up a large handful of Rotten Crispies and then stuffed them in her mouth.

Her face went purple, then pink, then green.

"BLEEEEECH!" she spluttered, spitting them out all over Mr Mossy.

"Peter, run and get Mrs Mossy something to drink!" shouted Mum.

Peter dashed to the kitchen and brought back a frothing drink.

"Thank you," gasped Mrs Mossy, taking the glass and gulping it down.

"YUCK!" she spluttered, spitting it out. "Are you trying to poison me, you horrible child?" she choked, flailing her arms and crashing into Dad, who had just walked in carrying the drinks tray.

CRASH! SPLASH!

Mum, Dad, Peter, and Mr and Mrs Mossy were soaked.

"Peter, what have you done?" shouted Mum.

Perfect Peter burst into tears and ran out of the room.

"Oh dear, I'm so sorry," said Mum.

"Never mind," said Mrs Mossy, through gritted teeth.

"Sit down, everyone," said Henry. "I'm going to do a show now."

93

"No," said Mum.

"No," said Dad.

"But Peter did one," howled Henry. "I WANT TO DO A SHOW!"

"All right," said Mum. "But just a quick one."

Henry sang. The guests held their ears.

"Not so loud, Henry," said Mum.

Henry pirouetted, trampling on the guests.

"Ooof," said Mr Mossy, clutching his toe.

"Aren't you finished, Henry?" said Dad.

Henry juggled, dropping both balls on Mrs Mossy's head.

"Ow," said Mrs Mossy.

"Now I'll show you my new karate moves," said Henry.

"NO!" shouted Mum and Dad.

But before anyone could stop him Henry's arms and legs flew out in a mad karate dance.

"HI-YA!" shrieked Henry, knocking into Mr Mossy.

Mr Mossy went flying across the room.

Whoosh! Off flew his toupee.

Click-clack! Out bounced his false teeth.

"Reginald!" gasped Mrs Mossy.
"Are you all right? Speak to me!"

"Uggghhh," groaned Mr Mossy.

"Isn't that great?" said Henry.
"Who wants to go next?"

"What's that terrible smell?"
choked Mrs Mossy.

"Oh no!" screamed Dad. "The
salmon is burning!"

Mum and Dad ran into the kitchen, followed by Mr and Mrs Mossy. Smoke poured from the oven. Mum grabbed a tea towel and started whacking the burning salmon.

WHACK! THWACK!

"Watch out!" screamed Dad.

The towel thwacked the bowl of chocolate mousse and sent it crashing to the ground.

SPLAT! There was chocolate mousse on the floor. There was chocolate mousse on the ceiling. And there was chocolate mousse all over Mr and Mrs Mossy, Mum, Dad and Henry.

"Oh no," said Mum, holding her head in her hands. Then she burst into tears. "What are we going to do?"

"Leave it to me, Mum," said Horrid Henry. He marched to the phone.

"Pizza Delight?" he said. "I'd like to order a mega-whopper, please."

HORRID HENRY

GETS RICH QUICK

(previously published as
Horrid Henry Strikes it Rich)

For Joshua and his classmates in 4H,
with thanks for all their help.

CONTENTS

1

HORRID HENRY RUNS AWAY

Horrid Henry was not having a good day. His younger brother, Perfect Peter, had grabbed the hammock first and wouldn't get out. Then Mum had ordered him to tidy his room just when he was watching *Rapper Zapper* on TV. And now Dad was yelling at him.

"What's the meaning of this letter, Henry?" shouted Dad.

"What letter?" snapped Henry. He was sick and tired of being nagged at.

"You know perfectly well what letter!" said Mum. "The letter from Miss Battle-Axe. The third this week."

Oh, *that* letter.

Dear Henry's Parents,
I am sorry to tell you that
today Henry:
Poked William
Tripped Linda
Shoved Dave
Pinched Andrew
Made rude noises, chewed gum,
and would not stop talking in class
Yours Sincerely
                    Boudicca Battle-Axe

Henry scowled.

"Can I help it if I have to burp?"

"And what about all the children you hurt?" said Dad.

"I hardly touched William. Linda got in my way, and Dave and Andrew annoyed me," said Henry. What a big fuss over nothing.

"Right," said Dad. "I am very disappointed with you. No TV, no comics and no sweets for a week."

"A WEEK!" screamed Henry. "For giving someone a little tap? It's not fair!"

"What about *my* letter?" said Peter.

Dear Peter's Parents
I am delighted to tell you that today Peter:
Helped Gordon
Shared with Sam
Volunteered to clean the paintbrushes, picked up the balls in P.E. and tidied the classroom without being asked.
Well done, Peter!
He is in the Good as Gold Book for the third time this month — a school record.
        Yours Sincerely
            Lydia Lovely

Dad glowed. "At least *one* child in this family knows how to behave."

Peter smiled modestly.

"You really should think more about other people, Henry," said Peter. "Then maybe one day *you'll* be in the Good as Gold Book."

Horrid Henry snarled and leapt on Peter. He was primordial slime oozing over a trapped insect.

"Yeowww!" howled Peter.

"Stop it, Henry!" shouted Mum. "Go straight to your room. NOW!"

Horrid Henry stomped upstairs to his bedroom and slammed the door.

"That's it!" screamed Henry. "No one in this family likes me so I'm leaving!"

He'd show his horrible parents. He would run away to the jungle. He would fight giant snakes, crush crocodiles and paddle alone up piranha-infested rivers, hacking his way through the vines. And

he'd never ever come back. Then they'd
be sorry. Serve them right for being so
mean to him.

He could see them now. If only we'd
been nicer to Henry, Dad would cry. Yes,
such a lovely boy, Mum would sob. Why
oh why were we so cruel to him? If only
Henry would come home he could
always have the hammock, Peter would
whimper. Why was I so selfish?

Shame really, thought Henry, dragging
his suitcase from under the bed, that I

won't be here to see them all wailing and gnashing their teeth.

Right, he thought, I'll only pack things I absolutely need. Lean and mean was the motto of Heroic Henry, Jungle Explorer.

Henry surveyed his room. What couldn't he live without?

He couldn't leave his Grisly Grub box and Dungeon Drink kit. Into the bag went the box and the kit. His Super Soaker 2000 water blaster would definitely come in handy in the wilds. And of course, lots of games in case he got bored fighting panthers.

Comics? Henry considered … definitely. He stuffed a big stack in his bag. A few packets of crisps and some sweets would be good. And the box of day-glo slime. Henry certainly didn't want Peter getting his sticky fingers on his precious slime. Teddy? Nah! Teddy wouldn't be any use where he was going.

Perfect, thought Henry. Then he
closed the bulging case. It would not
shut. Very reluctantly Henry took out
one comic and his football. There, he
thought. He'd be off at dawn. And
wouldn't they be sorry.

Tweet Tweet.

Heroic Henry, Jungle Explorer,
opened his eyes and leapt out of bed.
The early birds were chirping. It was
time to go. He flung on his jungle gear,

then sneaked into Peter's room. He crept over to Peter's bed and pinched him.

"Wha–wha," muttered Peter.

"Shut up and listen," whispered Henry fiercely. "I'm running away from home. If you tell anyone I've gone you'll be really sorry. In fact, you'll be dead."

"I won't tell," squeaked Peter.

"Good," said Henry. "And don't you dare touch anything in my room either."

Horrid Henry crept down the stairs.

BANG! BUMP! BANG! BUMP!

His suitcase clunked behind him. Henry froze. But no sound came from Mum and Dad's room.

At last Henry was safely down the stairs. Quietly he opened the back door and slipped into the misty garden.

He was outside. He was free! Goodbye civilization, thought Henry. Soon he'd be steaming down the Congo in search of adventure.

Of course I'll need a new name, thought Henry, as he began his long trek. To stop Mum and Dad tracking me down. Henry Intrepid sounded good. Piranha Pirate also had a nice ring. And

I'll need to disguise myself too, thought Henry. He'd wait until he got to the jungle for that. He stole a quick glance behind him. No search party was after him so far.

Henry walked, and walked, and walked. His suitcase got heavier, and heavier, and heavier.

Phew! Henry was getting a bit tired dragging that case.

I feel like I've been travelling for miles, thought Henry. I think I'll stop and have a little rest at that secret hideaway. No one will find me there.

Horrid Henry clambered into the tree-house and stepped on something squishy.

"AHHH!" screamed Henry.

"AHHH!" screamed the Squishy Thing.

"What are *you* doing here?" snapped Horrid Henry.

"What are *you* doing here?" snapped Moody Margaret.

"I've run away from home, if you must know," said Henry.

"So have I, and this is *my* tree-house," said Margaret. "Go away."

"I can sit here if I want to," said Henry, sitting down on Margaret's sleeping bag.

"Ouch! Get off my leg," said Margaret, pushing him off.

"And don't think for a minute I'll let

you come with me," said Henry.

"You can't come with me, either," said Margaret. "So where are *you* going?"

"The Congo," said Henry. He didn't know for sure exactly where that was, but he'd find it.

"Yuck," said Margaret. "Who'd want to go *there*? I'm going somewhere *much* better."

"Where, smarty pants?" asked Henry. He eyed Margaret's rather plentiful stash of biscuits.

"Susan's house," said Margaret.

Henry snorted.

"Susan's house? That's not running away."

"It is too," said Margaret.

"'Tisn't."

"'Tis."

"'Tisn't."

"'Tis. And I slept here all night," said Margaret. "Where did *you* sleep?"

Henry eyed the distance between

himself and Margaret's biscuits. Whistling nonchalantly, Henry stared in the opposite direction. Then, quick as a flash — SNATCH!

Henry grabbed a handful of biscuits and stuffed them in his mouth.

"Hey, that's my running-away food," said Margaret.

"Not any more," said Henry, snickering.

"Right," said Margaret. She grabbed his case and opened it. Then she hooted with laughter.

"That's all the food you brought?" she sneered. "I'd like to see you get to the jungle with that. And all those comics! I bet you didn't even bring a map."

"Oh yeah," said Henry. "What did *you* bring?"

Margaret opened her suitcase. Henry snorted with laughter.

"Clothes! I don't need clothes in the jungle. And anyway, *I* thought of running away first," jeered Henry.

"Didn't," said Margaret.

"Did," said Henry.

"I'm going to tell your mother where you are," said Margaret, "and then you'll be in big trouble."

"If you dare," said Henry, "I'll … I'll go straight over and tell yours. And I'll tell her you slept here last night. Won't you be in trouble then? In fact I'll go and tell her right now."

"I'll tell yours first," said Margaret.

They stood up, glaring at each other.

A faint, familiar smell drifted into the tree-house. It smelled like someone cooking.

Henry sniffed.

"What's that smell?"

Margaret sniffed.

"Pancakes," she said.

Pancakes! Only Henry's favourite breakfast.

"Whose house?"

Margaret sniffed again.

"Yours," she said sadly.

Yummy! Dad usually only made
pancakes on special occasions. What could
be happening? Then Henry had a terrible

thought. Could it be … they were *celebrating* his departure?

How dare they? Well, he'd soon put a stop to that.

Henry clambered out of the tree-house and ran home.

"Mum! Dad! I'm back!" he shouted. "Where are my pancakes?"

"They're all gone," said Mum.

All gone!

"Why didn't you call me?" said Henry. "You know I love pancakes."

"We did call you," said Mum, "but you didn't come down. We thought you didn't want any."

"But I wasn't here," wailed Henry. He glared at Peter. Perfect Peter went on eating his pancakes a little faster, his arm protecting his plate.

"Peter knew I wasn't here," said Henry. Then he lunged for Peter's plate. Peter screamed and held on tight.

118

"Henry said he'd kill me if I told so I didn't," shrieked Peter.

"Henry, let go of that plate and don't be so horrid to your brother!" said Dad.

Henry let go. There was only half a pancake left anyway and it had Peter's yucky germs all over it.

Dad sighed.

"All right, I'll make another batch," he said, getting up.

Henry was very surprised.

"Thanks, Dad," said Henry. He sat down at the table.

A big steaming stack of pancakes arrived. Henry poured lashings of maple syrup on top, then stuffed a huge forkful of buttery pancakes into his mouth.

Yummy!

He'd head for the Congo tomorrow.

HORRID HENRY'S SPORTS DAY

"We all want sports day to be a great success tomorrow," announced Miss Battle-Axe. "I am here to make sure that *no one*" – she glared at Horrid Henry – "spoils it."

Horrid Henry glared back. Horrid Henry hated sports day. Last year he hadn't won a single event. He'd dropped his egg in the egg-and-spoon race, tripped over Rude Ralph in the three-legged race, and collided with Sour Susan in the sack race. Henry's team had even lost the tug-of-war. Most sickening of all, Perfect Peter had won *both* his races.

If only the school had a sensible day,

like TV-watching day, or chocolate-eating day, or who could guzzle the most crisps day, Horrid Henry would be sure to win every prize. But no. *He* had to leap and dash about getting hot and bothered in front of stupid parents. When he became king he'd make teachers run all the races then behead the winners. King Henry the Horrible grinned happily.

"Pay attention, Henry!" barked Miss Battle-Axe. "What did I just say?"

Henry had no idea. "Sports day is cancelled?" he suggested hopefully.

Miss Battle-Axe fixed him with her steely eyes. "I said no one is to bring any sweets tomorrow. You'll all be given a delicious, refreshing piece of orange."

Henry slumped in his chair, scowling. All he could do was hope for rain.

Sports day dawned bright and sunny. Rats, thought Henry. He could, of course, pretend to be sick. But he'd tried that last year and Mum hadn't been fooled. The year before that he'd complained he'd hurt his leg. Unfortunately Dad then caught him dancing on the table.

It was no use. He'd just have to take part. If only he could win a race!

Perfect Peter bounced into his room.

"Sports day today!" beamed Peter. "And *I'm* responsible for bringing the hard-boiled eggs for the egg-and-spoon races. Isn't it exciting!"

"NO!" screeched Henry. "Get out of here!"

"But I only …" began Peter.

Henry leapt at him, roaring. He was a cowboy lassoing a runaway steer.

"Eeeaaargh!" squealed Peter.

"Stop being horrid, Henry!" shouted Dad. "Or no pocket money this week!"

Henry let Peter go.

"It's so unfair," he muttered, picking up his clothes from the floor and putting

them on. Why did he never win?

Henry reached under his bed and filled his pockets from the secret sweet tin he kept there. Horrid Henry was a master at eating sweets in school without being detected. At least he could scoff something good while the others were stuck eating dried-up old orange pieces.

Then he stomped downstairs. Perfect Peter was busy packing hard-boiled eggs into a carton.

Horrid Henry sat down scowling and gobbled his breakfast.

"Good luck, boys," said Mum. "I'll be there to cheer for you."

"Humph," growled Henry.

"Thanks, Mum," said Peter. "I expect I'll win my egg-and-spoon race again but of course it doesn't matter if I don't. It's *how* you play that counts."

"Shut up, Peter!" snarled Henry. Egg-and-spoon! Egg-and-spoon! If Henry heard that disgusting phrase once more he would start frothing at the mouth.

"Mum! Henry told me to shut up," wailed Peter, "and he attacked me this morning."

"Stop being horrid, Henry," said Mum. "Peter, come with me and we'll comb your hair. I want you to look your best when you win that trophy again."

Henry's blood boiled. He felt like snatching those eggs and hurling them against the wall.

Then Henry had a wonderful, spectac-

127

ular idea. It was so wonderful that …
Henry heard Mum coming back down
the stairs. There was no time to lose
crowing about his brilliance.

Horrid Henry ran to the fridge,
grabbed another egg carton and swapped
it for the box of hard-boiled ones on the
counter.

"Don't forget your eggs, Peter," said
Mum. She handed the carton to Peter,
who tucked it safely in his school bag.

Tee hee, thought Horrid Henry.

Henry's class lined up on the playing
fields. Flash! A small figure wearing
gleaming white trainers zipped by. It was
Aerobic Al, the fastest boy in Henry's class.

"Gotta run, gotta run, gotta run," he
chanted, gliding into place beside Henry.
"I will, of course, win every event," he
announced. "I've been training all year.

My dad's got a special place all ready for
my trophies."

"Who wants to race anyway?" sneered
Horrid Henry, sneaking a yummy
gummy fuzzball into his mouth.

"Now, teams for the three-legged
race," barked Miss Battle-Axe into her
megaphone. "This is a race showing how
well you co-operate and use teamwork
with your partner. Ralph will race with

William, Josh will race with Clare, Henry …" she glanced at her list, "… you will race with Margaret."

"NO!" screamed Horrid Henry.

"NO!" screamed Moody Margaret.

"Yes," said Miss Battle-Axe.

"But I want to be with Susan," said Margaret.

"No fussing," said Miss Battle-Axe. "Bert, where's your partner?"

"I dunno," said Beefy Bert.

Henry and Margaret stood as far apart as possible while their legs were tied together.

"You'd better do as I say, Henry," hissed Margaret. "*I'll* decide how we race."

"*I* will, you mean," hissed Henry.

"Ready … steady … GO!"

Miss Battle-Axe blew her whistle.

They were off! Henry moved to the left, Margaret moved to the right.

"This way, Henry!" shouted Margaret. She tried to drag him.

"No, this way!" shouted Henry. He tried to drag her.

They lurched wildly, left and right, then toppled over.

CRASH! Aerobic Al and Lazy Linda tripped over the screaming Henry and Margaret.

SMASH! Rude Ralph and Weepy William fell over Al and Linda.

BUMP! Dizzy Dave and Beefy Bert collided with Ralph and William.

"Waaa!" wailed Weepy William.

"It's all your fault, Margaret!" shouted Henry, pulling her hair.

"No, yours," shouted Margaret, pulling his harder.

Miss Battle-Axe blew her whistle frantically.

"Stop! Stop!" she ordered. "Henry! Margaret! What an example to set for the younger ones. Any more nonsense like that and you'll be severely punished. Everyone, get ready for the egg-and-spoon race!"

This was it! The moment Henry had been waiting for.

The children lined up in their teams. Moody Margaret, Sour Susan and Anxious Andrew were going first in

Henry's class. Henry glanced at Peter. Yes,
there he was, smiling proudly, next to
Goody-Goody Gordon, Spotless Sam,
and Tidy Ted. The eggs lay still on their
spoons. Horrid Henry held his breath.

"Ready … steady … GO!" shouted
Miss Battle-Axe.

They were off!

"Go Peter go!" shouted Mum.

Peter walked faster and faster and faster.

133

He was in the lead. He was pulling away from the field. Then … wobble … wobble … SPLAT!

"Aaaaagh!" yelped Peter.

Moody Margaret's egg wobbled.

SPLAT!

Then Susan's.

SPLAT!

Then everybody's.

SPLAT!

SPLAT!

SPLAT!

134

"I've got egg on my shoes!' wailed Margaret.

"I've ruined my new dress!" shrieked Susan.

"I've got egg all over me!" squealed Tidy Ted.

"Help!" squeaked Perfect Peter. Egg dripped down his trousers.

Parents surged forward, screaming and waving handkerchiefs and towels.

Rude Ralph and Horrid Henry shrieked with laughter.

Miss Battle-Axe blew her whistle.

"Who brought the eggs?" asked Miss Battle-Axe. Her voice was like ice.

"I did," said Perfect Peter. "But I brought hard-boiled ones."

"OUT!" shouted Miss Battle-Axe. "Out of the games!"

"But ... but ..." gasped Perfect Peter.

"No buts, out!" she glared. "Go straight to the Head."

Perfect Peter burst into tears and crept away.

Horrid Henry could hardly contain himself. This was the best sports day he'd ever been to.

"The rest of you, stop laughing at once. Parents, get back to your seats! Time for the next race!" ordered Miss Battle-Axe.

All things considered, thought Horrid Henry, lining up with his class, it hadn't been too terrible a day. He'd loved the egg-and-spoon race, of course. And he'd had fun pulling the other team into a muddy puddle in the tug-of-war, knocking over the obstacles in the obstacle race, and crashing into Aerobic Al in the sack race. But, oh, to actually win something!

There was just one race left before sports day was over. The cross-country run. The event Henry hated more than

any other. One long, sweaty, exhausting lap round the whole field.

Henry heaved his heavy bones to the starting line. His final chance to win … yet he knew there was no hope. If he beat Weepy William he'd be doing well.

Suddenly Henry had a wonderful, spectacular idea. Why had he never thought of this before? Truly, he was a genius. Wasn't there some ancient Greek who'd won a race by throwing down golden apples which his rival kept stopping to pick up? Couldn't he, Henry, learn something from those old Greeks?

"Ready … steady … GO!" shrieked Miss Battle-Axe.

Off they dashed.

"Go, Al, go!" yelled his father.

"Get a move on, Margaret!" shrieked her mother.

"Go Ralph!" cheered his father.

"Do your best, Henry," said Mum.

Horrid Henry reached into his pocket and hurled some sweets. They thudded to the ground in front of the runners.

"Look, sweets!" shouted Henry.

Al checked behind him. He was well in the lead. He paused and scooped up one sweet, and then another. He glanced behind again, then started unwrapping the yummy gummy fuzzball.

"Sweets!" yelped Greedy Graham. He stopped to pick up as many as he could

find then stuffed them in his mouth.

"Yummy!" screamed Graham.

"Sweets! Where?" chanted the others. Then they stopped to look.

"Over there!" yelled Henry, throwing another handful. The racers paused to pounce on the treats.

While the others munched and crunched, Henry made a frantic dash for the lead.

He was out in front! Henry's legs moved as they had never moved before, pounding round the field. And there was the finishing line!

THUD! THUD! THUD! Henry glanced back. Oh no! Aerobic Al was catching up!

Henry felt in his pocket. He had one giant gob-stopper left. He looked round, panting.

"Go home and take a nap, Henry!" shouted Al, sticking out his tongue as he raced past.

Henry threw down the gob-stopper in front of Al. Aerobic Al hesitated, then skidded to a halt and picked it up. He could beat Henry any day so why not show off a bit?

Suddenly Henry sprinted past. Aerobic Al dashed after him. Harder and harder, faster and faster Henry ran. He was a bird. He was a plane. He flew across the finishing line.

"The winner is … Henry?" squeaked

Miss Battle-Axe.

"I've been robbed!" screamed Aerobic Al.

"Hurray!" yelled Henry.

Wow, what a great day, thought Horrid Henry, proudly carrying home his trophy. Al's dad shouting at Miss Battle-Axe and Mum. Miss Battle-Axe and Mum shouting back. Peter sent off in disgrace. And he, Henry, the big winner.

"I can't think how you got those eggs muddled up," said Mum.

"Me neither," said Perfect Peter, sniffling.

"Never mind, Peter," said Henry brightly. "It's not winning, it's *how* you play that counts."

3

HORRID HENRY
GETS RICH QUICK

Horrid Henry loved money. He loved counting money. He loved holding money. He loved spending money. There was only one problem. Horrid Henry never had any money.

He sat on his bedroom floor and rattled his empty skeleton bank. How his mean parents expected him to get by on 50p a week pocket money he would never know. It was so unfair! Why should they have all the money when there were so many things *he* needed? Comic books. Whopper chocolate bars. A new football. More knights for his castle. Horrid Henry looked round his room, scowling.

True, his shelves were filled with toys, but nothing he still wanted to play with.

"MUM!" screamed Henry.

"Stop shouting, Henry," shouted Mum. "If you have something to say come downstairs and say it."

"I need more pocket money," said Henry. "Ralph gets a pound a week."

"Different children get different amounts," said Mum. "I think 50p a week is perfectly adequate."

"Well I don't," said Henry.

"I'm very happy with *my* pocket money, Mum," said Perfect Peter. "I always save loads from my 30p. After all, if you look after the pennies the pounds will look after themselves."

"Quite right, Peter," said Mum, smiling.

Henry walked slowly past Peter. When Mum wasn't looking he reached out and grabbed him. He was a giant crab crushing a prawn in its claws.

"OWWW!" wailed Peter. "Henry pinched me!"

"I did not," said Henry.

"No pocket money for a week, Henry," said Mum.

"That's not fair!" howled Henry. "I need money!"

"You'll just have to save more," said Mum.

"No!" shouted Henry. He hated saving money.

"Then you'll have to find a way to earn some," said Mum.

Earn? Earn money? Suddenly Henry

had a brilliant, fantastic idea.

"Mum, can I set up a stall and sell some stuff I don't want?"

"Like what?" said Mum.

"You know, old toys, comics, games, things I don't use any more," said Henry.

Mum hesitated for a moment. She couldn't think of anything wrong with selling off old junk.

"All right," said Mum.

"Can I help, Henry?" said Peter.

"No way," said Henry.

"Oh please," said Peter.

"Stop being horrid, Henry, and let Peter help you," said Mum, "or no stall."

"OK," said Henry, scowling, "you can make the For Sale signs."

Horrid Henry ran to his bedroom and piled his unwanted jumble into a box. He cleared his shelves of books, his wardrobe of party clothes, and his toy-box of puzzles with pieces missing.

Then Horrid Henry paused. To make big money he definitely needed a few more valuable items. Now, where could he find some?

Henry crept into Peter's room. He could sell Peter's stamp collection, or his nature kit. Nah, thought Henry, no-one would want that boring stuff.

Then Henry glanced inside Mum and Dad's room. It was packed with rich pickings. Henry sauntered over to Mum's dressing table. Look at all that perfume, thought Henry, she wouldn't miss one bottle. He chose a large crystal bottle

with a swan-shaped stopper and packed
it in the box. Now, what other jumble
could he find?

Aha! There was Dad's tennis racket.
Dad never played tennis. That racket was
just lying there collecting dust when it
could go to a much better home.

Perfect, thought Henry, adding the
racket to his collection. Then he staggered
out to the pavement to set up the display.

Horrid Henry surveyed his stall. It was
piled high with great bargains. He should
make a fortune.

"But Henry," said Peter, looking up
from drawing a sign, "that's Dad's tennis
racket. Are you sure he wants you to
sell it?"

"Of course I'm sure, stupid," snapped
Henry. If only he could get rid of his
horrible brother wouldn't life be perfect.

Then Horrid Henry looked at Peter. What was it the Romans did with their leftover captives? Hmmn, he thought. He looked again. Hmmmn, he thought.

"Peter," said Henry sweetly, "how would you like to earn some money?"

"Oh yes!" said Peter. "How?"

"We could sell you as a slave."

Perfect Peter thought for a moment. "How much would I get?"

"10p," said Henry.

"Wow," said Peter. "That means I'll have £6.47 in my piggybank. Can I wear a For Sale sign?"

"Certainly," said Horrid Henry. He scribbled: For Sale £5, then placed the sign round Peter's neck.

"Now look smart," said Henry. "I see some customers coming."

"What's going on?" said Moody Margaret.

"Yeah, Henry, what are you doing?" said Sour Susan.

"I'm having a jumble sale," said Henry. "Lots of bargains. All the money raised will go to a very good cause."

"What's that?" said Susan.

"Children in Need," said Henry. I am a child and I'm certainly in need so that's true, he thought.

Moody Margaret picked up a punctured football.

"Bargain? This is just a lot of old junk."

"No it isn't," said Henry. "Look. Puzzles, books, perfume, stuffed toys, *and* a slave."

Moody Margaret looked up.

"I could use a good slave," said Margaret. "I'll give you 25p for him."

"25p for an excellent slave? He's worth at least £1.50."

"Make a muscle, slave," said Moody Margaret.

Perfect Peter made a muscle.

"Hmmn," said Margaret. "50p is my final offer."

"Done," said Horrid Henry. Why had he never thought of selling Peter before?

"How come I get 10p when I cost 50p?" said Peter.

"Shopkeeper's expenses," said Henry. "Now run along with your new owner."

Business was brisk.

Rude Ralph bought some football cards.

Sour Susan bought Best Bear and Mum's perfume.

Beefy Bert bought a racing car with three wheels.

Then Aerobic Al jogged by.

"Cool racket," he said, picking up Dad's racket and giving it a few swings. "How much?"

"£10," said Henry.

"I'll give you £2," said Al.

£2! That was more money than Horrid Henry had ever had in his life! He was rich!

"Done," said Henry.

Horrid Henry sat in the sitting room gazing happily at his stacks of money. £3.12! Boy, would that buy a lot of chocolate! Mum came into the room.

"Henry, have you seen my new perfume? You know, the one with the swan on top."

"No," said Henry. Yikes, he never thought she would notice.

"And where's Peter?" said Mum.

155

"I thought he was playing with you."

"He's gone," said Henry.

Mum stared at him.

"What do you mean, gone?"

"Gone," said Henry, popping a crisp into his mouth. "I sold him."

"You did what?" whispered Mum. Her face was pale.

"You said I could sell anything I didn't want, and I certainly didn't want Peter, so I sold him to Margaret."

Mum's jaw dropped.

"You go straight over to Margaret's and buy him back!" screamed Mum. "You horrid boy! Selling your own brother!"

"But I don't want him back," said Henry.

"No ifs or buts, Henry!" screeched Mum. "You just get your brother back."

"I can't afford to buy him," said Horrid Henry. "If you want him back you should pay for him."

"HENRY!" bellowed Mum.

"All right," grumbled Henry, getting to his feet. He sighed. What a waste of good money, he thought, climbing over the wall into Margaret's garden.

Margaret was lying by the paddling pool.

"SLAVE!" she ordered. "I'm hot! Fan me!"

Perfect Peter came out of her house carrying a large fan.

He started to wave it in Moody Margaret's direction.

"Faster, slave!" said Margaret.

Peter fanned faster.

"Slower, slave!" said Margaret.

Peter fanned slower.

"Slave! A cool drink, and make it snappy!" ordered Margaret.

Horrid Henry followed Peter back into the kitchen.

"Henry!" squeaked Peter. "Have you come to rescue me?"

"No," said Henry.

"Please," said Peter. "I'll do anything. You can have the 10p."

The cash register in Henry's head started to whirl.

"Not enough," said Henry.

"I'll give you 50p. I'll give you a pound. I'll give you £2.00," said Peter.

"She's horrible. She's even worse than you."

"Right, you can stay here for ever," said Henry.

"Sorry, Henry," said Perfect Peter. "You're the best brother in the world. I'll give you all my money."

Horrid Henry looked as if he were considering this offer.

"All right, wait here," said Henry. "I'll see what I can do."

"Thank you, Henry," said Peter.

Horrid Henry went back into the garden.

"Where's my drink?" said Margaret.

"My mum says I have to have Peter back," said Henry.

Moody Margaret gazed at him.

"Oh yeah?"

"Yeah," said Henry.

"Well I don't want to sell him," said Margaret. "I paid good money for him."

Henry had hoped she'd forgotten that.

"OK, here's the 50p," he said.

Moody Margaret lay back and closed her eyes.

"I haven't spent all this time and effort training him just to get my money back," she said. "He's worth at least £10 now."

Slowly Henry stuck his hand back into his pocket.

"75p and that's my final offer."

Moody Margaret knew a good deal when she was offered one.

"OK," she said. "Give me my money."

Reluctantly, Henry paid her. But that still leaves over £2, thought Henry, so I'm well ahead.

Then he went in to fetch Peter.

"You cost me £6.00," he said.

"Thank you, Henry," said Peter. "I'll pay you as soon as we get home."

Yippee! thought Horrid Henry. I'm super rich! The world is mine!

Clink, clank, clink, went Henry's heavy pockets as Henry did his money dance.

"CLINK, CLANK, CLINK,
I'm rich, I'm rich, I'm rich,
I'm rich as I can be,"

sang Henry.

Spend, spend, spend would be his motto from now on.

"Hello everybody," called Dad, coming through the front door. "What a lovely afternoon! Anyone for tennis?"

4

HORRID HENRY'S CHRISTMAS

Perfect Peter sat on the sofa looking through the Toy Heaven catalogue. Henry had hogged it all morning to write his Christmas present list. Naturally, this was not a list of the presents Henry planned to give. This was a list of what he wanted to get.

Horrid Henry looked up from his work. He'd got a bit stuck after: a million pounds, a parrot, a machete, swimming pool, trampoline, and Killer Catapult.

"Gimme that!" shouted Horrid Henry. He snatched the Toy Heaven catalogue from Perfect Peter.

"You give that back!" shouted Peter.

"It's my turn!" shouted Henry.

"You've had it the whole morning!" shrieked Peter. "Mum!"

"Stop being horrid, Henry," said Mum, running in from the kitchen.

Henry ignored her. His eyes were glued to the catalogue. He'd found it. The toy of his dreams. The toy he had to have.

"I want a Boom-Boom Basher," said Henry. It was a brilliant toy which crashed into everything, an ear-piercing siren wailing all the while. Plus all the trasher attachments. Just the thing for knocking down Perfect Peter's marble run.

"I've got to have a Boom-Boom Basher," said Henry, adding it to his list in big letters.

"Absolutely not, Henry," said Mum. "I will not have that horrible noisy toy in my house."

"Aw, come on," said Henry. "Pleeease."

166

Dad came in.

"I want a Boom-Boom Basher for Christmas," said Henry.

"No way," said Dad. "Too expensive."

"You are the meanest, most horrible parents in the whole world," screamed Henry. "I hate you! I want a Boom-Boom Basher!"

"That's no way to ask, Henry," said Perfect Peter. "I want doesn't get."

Henry lunged at Peter. He was an octopus squeezing the life out of the helpless fish trapped in its tentacles.

"Help," spluttered Peter.

"Stop being horrid, Henry, or I'll cancel the visit to Father Christmas," shouted Mum.

Henry stopped.

The smell of burning mince pies drifted into the room.

"Ahh, my pies!" shrieked Mum.

*

167

"How much longer are we going to have to wait?" whined Henry. "I'm sick of this!"

Horrid Henry, Perfect Peter, and Mum were standing near the end of a very long queue waiting to see Father Christmas. They had been waiting for a very long time.

"Oh, Henry, isn't this exciting," said Peter. "A chance to meet Father Christmas. I don't mind how long I wait."

"Well I do," snapped Henry. He began to squirm his way through the crowd.

"Hey, stop pushing!" shouted Dizzy Dave.

"Wait your turn!" shouted Moody Margaret.

"I was here first!" shouted Lazy Linda.

Henry shoved his way in beside Rude Ralph.

"What are you asking Father Christmas for?" said Henry. "I want a Boom-Boom Basher."

"Me too," said Ralph. "And a Goo-Shooter."

Henry's ears pricked up.

"What's that?"

"It's really cool," said Ralph. "It splatters green goo over everything and every-body."

"Yeah!" said Horrid Henry as Mum dragged him back to his former place in the queue.

*

169

"What do you want for Christmas, Graham?" asked Santa.

"Sweets!" said Greedy Graham.

"What do you want for Christmas, Bert?" asked Santa.

"I dunno," said Beefy Bert.

"What do you want for Christmas, Peter?" asked Santa.

"A dictionary!" said Peter. "Stamps, seeds, a geometry kit, and some cello music, please."

"No toys?"

"No thank you," said Peter. "I have plenty of toys already. Here's a present for you, Santa," he added, holding out a beautifully wrapped package. "I made it myself."

"What a delightful young man," said Santa. Mum beamed proudly.

"My turn now," said Henry, pushing Peter off Santa's lap.

"And what do you want for Christmas, Henry?" asked Santa.

Henry unrolled the list.

"I want a Boom–Boom Basher and a Goo-Shooter," said Henry.

"Well, we'll see about that," said Santa.

"Great!" said Henry. When grown-ups said "We'll see," that almost always meant "Yes."

It was Christmas Eve.

Mum and Dad were rushing around the house tidying up as fast as they could.

Perfect Peter was watching a nature programme on TV.

"I want to watch cartoons!" said

171

Henry. He grabbed the clicker and switched channels.

"I was watching the nature programme!" said Peter. "Mum!"

"Stop it, Henry," muttered Dad. "Now, both of you, help tidy up before your aunt and cousin arrive."

Perfect Peter jumped up to help.

Horrid Henry didn't move.

"Do they have to come?" said Henry.

"Yes," said Mum.

"I hate cousin Steve," said Henry.

"No you don't," said Mum.

"I do too," snarled Henry. If there was a yuckier person walking the earth than Stuck-up Steve, Henry had yet to meet him. It was the one bad thing about Christmas, having him come to stay every year.

Ding Dong. It must be Rich Aunt Ruby and his horrible cousin. Henry watched as his aunt staggered in carrying boxes and boxes of presents which she dropped under the brightly-lit tree. Most of them, no doubt, for Stuck-up Steve.

"I wish we weren't here," moaned Stuck-up Steve. "Our house is so much nicer."

"Shh," said Rich Aunt Ruby. She went off with Henry's parents.

Stuck-up Steve looked down at Henry.

"Bet I'll get loads more presents than you," he said.

"Bet you won't," said Henry, trying to sound convinced.

"It's not what you get it's the thought that counts," said Perfect Peter.

"*I'm* getting a Boom-Boom Basher *and* a Goo-Shooter," said Stuck-up Steve.

"So am I," said Henry.

"Nah," said Steve. "You'll just get horrible presents like socks and stuff. And won't I laugh."

When I'm king, thought Henry, I'll

have a snake pit made just for Steve.

"I'm richer than you," boasted Steve. "And I've got loads more toys." He looked at the Christmas tree.

"Call that twig a tree?" sneered Steve. "Ours is so big it touches the ceiling."

"Bedtime, boys," called Dad. "And remember, no one is to open any presents until we've eaten lunch and gone for a walk."

"Good idea, Dad," said Perfect Peter. "It's always nice to have some fresh air on Christmas Day and leave the presents for later."

Ha, thought Horrid Henry. We'll see about that.

The house was dark. The only noise was the rasping sound of Stuck-up Steve, snoring away in his sleeping bag.

Horrid Henry could not sleep. Was

there a Boom-Boom Basher waiting for him downstairs?

He rolled over on his side and tried to get comfortable. It was no use. How could he live until Christmas morning?

Horrid Henry could bear it no longer. He had to find out if he'd been given a Boom-Boom Basher.

Henry crept out of bed, grabbed his torch, stepped over Stuck-up Steve – resisting the urge to stomp on him – and sneaked down the stairs.

CR-EEAK went the creaky stair. Henry froze.

The house was silent.

Henry tiptoed into the dark sitting room. There was the tree. And there were all the presents, loads and loads and loads of them!

Right, thought Henry, I'll just have a quick look for my Boom-Boom Basher and then get straight back to bed.

He seized a giant package. This looked promising. He gave it a shake. Thud-thud-thunk. This sounds good, thought Henry. His heart leapt. I just know it's a Boom-Boom Basher. Then he checked the label: "Merry Christmas, Steve."

Rats, thought Henry.

He shook another temptingly-shaped present: "Merry Christmas, Steve." And another: "Merry Christmas, Steve." And another. And another.

Then Henry felt a small, soft, squishy package. Socks for sure. I hope it's not for me, he thought. He checked the label: "Merry Christmas, Henry."

There must be some mistake, thought Henry. Steve needs socks more than I do. In fact, I'd be doing him a favour giving them to him.

Switch! It was the work of a moment to swap labels.

Now, let's see, thought Henry. He eyed a Goo-Shooter shaped package with Steve's name on it, then found another, definitely book-shaped one, intended for himself.

Switch!

Come to think of it, Steve had far too many toys cluttering up his house. Henry had heard Aunt Ruby complaining about the mess just tonight.

Switch! Switch! Switch! Then Horrid Henry crept back to bed.

It was 6:00 a.m.

"Merry Christmas!" shouted Henry. "Time to open the presents!"

Before anyone could stop him Henry thundered downstairs.

Stuck-up Steve jumped up and followed him.

"Wait!" shouted Mum.

"Wait!" shouted Dad.

The boys dashed into the sitting room and flung themselves upon the presents. The room was filled with shrieks of delight and howls of dismay as they tore off the wrapping paper.

"Socks!" screamed Stuck-up Steve. "What a crummy present! Thanks for nothing!"

"Don't be so rude, Steve," said Rich Aunt Ruby, yawning.

"A Goo-Shooter!" shouted Horrid Henry. "Wow! Just what I wanted!"

"A geometry set," said Perfect Peter. "Great!"

"A flower-growing kit?" howled Stuck-up Steve. "Phooey!"

"Make Your Own Fireworks!" beamed Henry. "Wow!"

"Tangerines!" screamed Stuck-up Steve. "This is the worst Christmas ever!"

"A Boom-Boom Basher!" beamed

Henry. "Gee, thanks. Just what I wanted!"

"Let me see that label," snarled Steve.
He grabbed the torn wrapping paper.
"Merry Christmas, Henry," read the
label. There was no mistake.

"Where's *my* Boom-Boom Basher?" screamed Steve.

"It must be here somewhere," said Aunt Ruby.

"Ruby, you shouldn't have bought one for Henry," said Mum, frowning.

"I didn't," said Ruby.

Mum looked at Dad.

"Nor me," said Dad.

"Nor me," said Mum.

"Father Christmas gave it to me," said

Horrid Henry. "I asked him to and he did."

Silence.

"He's got my presents!" screamed Steve. "I want them back!"

"They're mine!" screamed Henry, clutching his booty. "Father Christmas gave them to me."

"No, mine!" screamed Steve.

Aunt Ruby inspected the labels. Then she looked grimly at the two howling boys.

"Perhaps I made a mistake when I labelled some of the presents," she muttered to Mum. "Never mind. We'll sort it out later," she said to Steve.

"It's not fair!" howled Steve.

"Why don't you try on your new socks?" said Horrid Henry.

Stuck-up Steve lunged at Henry. But Henry was ready for him.

SPLAT!

"Aaaarggh!" screamed Steve, green goo dripping from his face and clothes and hair.

"HENRY!" screamed Mum and Dad. "How could you be so horrid!"

"Boom-Boom CRASH! NEE NAW NEE NAW WHOO WHOOO WHOOO!"

What a great Christmas, thought Henry, as his Boom-Boom Basher knocked over Peter's marble run.

"Say goodbye to Aunt Ruby, Henry," said Mum. She looked tired.

Rich Aunt Ruby and Steve had decided to leave a little earlier than planned.

"Goodbye, Aunt," said Henry. "Goodbye, Steve. Can't wait to see you next Christmas."

"Actually," said Mum, "you're staying the night next month."

Uh-oh, thought Horrid Henry.

HORRiD HENRY'S
HAUNTED HOUSE

For Mary Gibson,
Head teacher, Yerbury School.
And for Joshua,
who always has such brilliant ideas,
with love and thanks

CONTENTS

1

HORRID HENRY

AND THE
COMFY BLACK CHAIR

Ah, Saturday! Best day of the week, thought Horrid Henry, flinging off the covers and leaping out of bed. No school! No homework! A day of TV heaven! Mum and Dad liked sleeping in on a Saturday. So long as Henry and Peter were quiet they could watch TV until Mum and Dad woke up.

Horrid Henry could picture it now. He would stretch out in the comfy black chair, grab the remote control, and switch on the TV. All his favourite shows were on today: *Rapper Zapper, Mutant*

Max, and *Gross-Out*. If he hurried he would be just in time for *Rapper Zapper*.

He thudded down the stairs and flung open the sitting room door. A horrible sight met his eyes.

There, stretched out on the comfy black chair and clutching the remote control, was his younger brother, Perfect Peter.

Henry gasped. How could this be? Henry always got downstairs first. The TV was already on. But it was not switched to *Rapper Zapper*. A terrible

tinkly tune trickled out of the TV.
Oh no! It was the world's most boring
show, *Daffy and her Dancing Daisies*.

"Switch the channel!" ordered Henry.
"*Rapper Zapper*'s on."

"That's a horrid, nasty programme,"
said Perfect Peter, shuddering. He held
tight to the remote.

"I said switch the channel!" hissed
Henry.

"I won't!" said Peter. "You know the
rules. The first one downstairs gets to sit
in the comfy black chair and decides
what to watch. And I want to watch
Daffy."

Henry could hardly believe his ears.
Perfect Peter was ... refusing to obey an
order?

"NO!" screamed Henry. "I hate that
show. I want to watch Rapper Zapper!"

"Well, I want to watch Daffy," said
Perfect Peter.

"But that's a baby show," said Henry.

"Dance, my daisies, dance!" squealed the revolting Daffy.

"La, la la la la!" trilled the daisies.

"La, la la la la!" sang Peter.

"Baby, baby!" taunted Henry. If only he could get Peter to run upstairs crying then *he* could get the chair.

"Peter is a baby, Peter is a baby!" jeered Henry.

Peter kept his eyes glued to the screen.

Horrid Henry could stand it no longer. He pounced on Peter, snatched the remote, and pushed Peter onto the floor. He was Rapper Zapper liquidating a pesky android.

"AAAAAH!" screamed Perfect Peter. "MUUUMMM!"

Horrid Henry leaped into the comfy black chair and switched channels.

"Grrrrrrr!" growled Rapper Zapper, blasting a baddie.

"DON'T BE HORRID, HENRY!" shouted Mum, storming through the door. "GO TO YOUR ROOM!"

"NOOOO!" wailed Henry. "Peter started it!"

"NOW!" screamed Mum.

"La, la la la la!" trilled the Daisies.

★

BUZZZZZZZZ.

Horrid Henry switched off the alarm.
It was six a.m. the following Saturday.
Henry was taking no chances. Even if
he had to grit his teeth and watch
Rise and Shine before *Gross-Out* started
it was worth it. And he'd seen the
coming attractions for today's *Gross-Out*:
who could eat the most cherry pie in
five minutes while blasting the other
contestants with a goo-shooter. Henry
couldn't wait.

There was no sound from Peter's
room. Ha, ha, thought Henry. He'll have
to sit on the lumpy sofa and watch what
I want to watch.

Horrid Henry skipped into the sitting
room. And stopped.

"Remember, children, always eat with
a knife and fork!" beamed a cheerful
presenter. It was *Manners with Maggie*.
There was Perfect Peter in his slippers

and dressing gown, stretched out on
the comfy black chair. Horrid Henry
felt sick. Another Saturday ruined!
He had to watch *Gross-Out*! He just
had to.

Horrid Henry was just about to push
Peter off the chair when he stopped.
Suddenly he had a brilliant idea.

"Peter! Mum and Dad want to see
you. They said it's urgent!"

Perfect Peter leaped off the comfy
black chair and dashed upstairs.

Tee hee, thought Horrid Henry.
ZAP!

"Welcome to *GROSS-OUT!*"
shrieked the presenter, Marvin the
Maniac. "Boy, will you all be feeling sick
today! It's GROSS! GROSS! GROSS!"

"Yeah!" said Horrid Henry. This was
great!

Perfect Peter reappeared.

"They didn't want me," said Peter.
"And they're cross because I woke them
up."

"They told me they did," said Henry,
eyes glued to the screen.

Peter stood still.

"Please give me the chair back,
Henry."

Henry didn't answer.

"I had it first," said Peter.

"Shut up, I'm trying to watch," said
Henry.

"Ewwwwww, gross!" screamed the TV
audience.

"I was watching *Manners with Maggie*,"

said Peter. "She's showing how to eat soup without slurping."

"Tough," said Henry. "Oh, gross!" he chortled, pointing at the screen.

Peter hid his eyes.

"Muuuuummmmmmmmm!" shouted Peter. "Henry's being mean to me!"

Mum appeared in the doorway.

She looked furious.

"Henry, go to your room!" shouted Mum. "We were trying to sleep. Is it too much to ask to be left in peace one morning a week?"

"But Peter —"

Mum pointed to the door.

"Out!" said Mum.

"It's not fair!" howled Henry, stomping off.

ZAP!

"And now Kate, our guest manners expert, will demonstrate the proper way to butter toast."

Henry slammed the door behind him as hard as he could. Peter had got the comfy black chair for the very last time.

BUZZZZZZZ.

Horrid Henry switched off the alarm. It was two a.m. the *following* Saturday.

The *Gross-Out* Championships were on
in the morning. He grabbed his pillow
and duvet and sneaked out of the room.
He was taking no chances. Tonight he
would *sleep* in the comfy black chair.
After all, Mum and Dad had never
said how *early* he could get up.

Henry tiptoed out of his room into
the hall.

All quiet in Peter's room.

All quiet in Mum and Dad's.

Henry crept down the stairs and
carefully opened the sitting room door.
The room was pitch black. Better not
turn on the light, thought Henry. He
felt his way along the wall until his
fingers touched the back of the comfy
black chair. He felt around the top. Ah,
there was the remote. He'd sleep with
that under his pillow, just to be safe.

Henry flung himself onto the chair
and landed on something lumpy.

"AHHHHHHHHH!" screamed Henry.

"AHHHHHHHHH!" screamed the Lump.

"HELP!" screamed Henry and the Lump.

Feet pounded down the stairs.

"What's going on down there?" shouted Dad, switching on the light.

Henry blinked.

"Henry jumped on my head!" snivelled a familiar voice beneath him.

"Henry, what are you doing?" said Dad. "It's two o'clock in the morning!"

Henry's brain whirled. "I thought I heard a burglar so I crept down to keep watch."

"Henry's lying!" said Peter, sitting up. "He came down because he wanted the comfy black chair."

"Liar!" said Henry. "And what were *you* doing down here?"

"I couldn't sleep and I didn't want to wake you, Dad," said Peter. "So I came down as quietly as I could to get a drink of water. Then I felt sleepy and lay down for a moment. I'm very sorry, Dad, it will never happen again."

"All right," said Dad, stifling a yawn. "From now on, you are not to come down here before seven a.m. or there will be no TV for a week! Is that clear?"

"Yes, Dad," said Peter.

"Yeah," muttered Henry.

He glared at Perfect Peter.

Perfect Peter glared at Horrid Henry. Then they both went upstairs to their bedrooms and closed the doors.

"Goodnight!" called Henry cheerfully. "My, I'm sleepy."

But Henry did not go to bed. He needed to think.

He *could* wait until everyone was asleep and sneak back down. But what if he got caught? No TV for a week would be unbearable.

But what if he missed the *Gross-Out* Championships? And never found out if Tank Thomas or Tapioca Tina won the day? Henry shuddered. There had to be a better way.

Ahh! He had it! He would set his clock ahead and make sure he was first down. Brilliant! *Gross-Out* here I come, he thought.

But wait. What if Peter had the *same* brilliant idea? That would spoil everything. Henry had to double-check.

Henry opened his bedroom door. The coast was clear. He tiptoed out and sneaked into Peter's room.

There was Peter, sound asleep. And there was his clock. Peter hadn't changed the time. Phew.

And then Henry had a truly wicked idea. It was so evil, and so horrid, that for a moment even he hesitated. But hadn't Peter been horrible and selfish, stopping Henry watching his favourite shows? He certainly had. And wouldn't it be great if Peter got into trouble, just for once?

Perfect Peter rolled over. "La, la la la la," he warbled in his sleep.

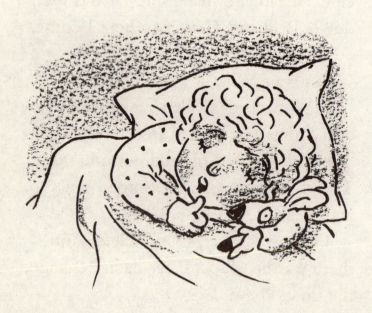

That did it. Horrid Henry moved Peter's clock an hour ahead. Then Henry sneaked downstairs and turned up the TV's volume as loud as it would go. Finally, he opened Mum and Dad's door, and crept back to bed.

"IT'S GROW AND SHOW! THE VEGETABLE SHOW FOR TINIES! JUST LOOK AT ALL THESE LOVELY VEGETABLES!"

The terrible noise boomed through the house, blasting Henry out of bed.

"HENRY!" bellowed Dad. "Come here this instant!"

Henry sauntered into his parents' bedroom.

"What is it?" he asked, yawning loudly.

Mum and Dad looked confused.

"Wasn't that you watching TV downstairs?"

"No," said Henry, stretching. "I was asleep."

Mum looked at Dad.

Dad looked at Mum.

"You mean *Peter* is downstairs watching TV at six a.m.?"

Henry shrugged.

"Send Peter up here this minute!" said Dad.

For once Henry did not need to be asked twice. He ran downstairs and burst into the sitting room.

"I grew carrots!"

"I grew string beans!"

"Peter! Mum and Dad want to see you right away!" said Henry.

Peter didn't look away from *Grow and Show*.

"PETER! Dad asked me to send you up!"

"You're just trying to trick me," said Peter.

"You'd better go or you'll be in big trouble," said Henry.

"Fool me once, shame on you. Fool me twice, shame on me," said Peter. "I'm not moving."

"Now, just look at all these beautiful tomatoes Timmy's grown," squealed the TV.

"Wow," said Peter.

"Don't say I didn't warn you," said Henry.

"PETER!" bellowed Dad. "NO TV FOR A MONTH! COME HERE THIS MINUTE!"

Perfect Peter burst into tears. He jumped from the chair and crept out of the room.

Horrid Henry sauntered over to the comfy black chair and stretched out. He picked up the remote and switched channels.

ZAP!

Rapper Zapper stormed into the spaceship and pulverized some alien slime.

"Way to go, Rapper Zapper!" shrieked Horrid Henry. Soon *Gross-Out* would be on. Wasn't life sweet?

2

HORRID HENRY'S
HAUNTED HOUSE

"No way!" shrieked Horrid Henry.
He was not staying the weekend with
his slimy cousin Stuck-Up Steve, and
that was that. He sat in the back seat
of the car with his arms folded.

"Yes you are," said Mum.

"Steve can't wait to see you,' said Dad.

This was not exactly true. After Henry
had sprayed Steve with green goo last
Christmas, *and* helped himself to a few of
Steve's presents, Steve had sworn revenge.
Under the circumstances, Henry thought
it would be a good idea to keep out of
Steve's way.

And now Mum had arranged for him to spend the weekend while she and Dad went off on their own! Perfect Peter was staying with Tidy Ted, and he was stuck with Steve.

"It's a great chance for you boys to become good friends," she said. "Steve is a very nice boy."

"I feel sick," said Henry, coughing.

"Stop faking," said Mum. "You were well enough to play football all morning."

"I'm too tired," said Henry, yawning.

"I'm sure you'll get plenty of rest at Aunt Ruby's," said Dad firmly.

"I'M NOT GOING!" howled Henry.

Mum and Dad took Henry by the arms, dragged him to Rich Aunt Ruby's door, and rang the bell.

The massive door opened immediately.

"Welcome, Henry," said Rich Aunt

Ruby, giving him a great smacking kiss.

"Henry, how lovely to see you," said Stuck-Up Steve sweetly. "That's a very nice second-hand jumper you're wearing."

"Hush, Steve," said Rich Aunt Ruby. "I think Henry looks very smart."

Henry glared at Steve. Thank goodness he'd remembered his Goo-Shooter. He had a feeling he might need it.

"Goodbye, Henry," said Mum. "Be good. Ruby, thank you so much for having him."

"Our pleasure," lied Aunt Ruby.

The great door closed.

Henry was alone in the house with his arch-enemy.

Henry looked grimly at Steve. What a horrible boy, he thought.

Steve looked grimly at Henry. What a horrible boy, he thought.

"Why don't you both go upstairs and play in Steve's room till supper's ready?" said Aunt Ruby.

"I'll show Henry where he's sleeping first," said Steve.

"Good idea," said Aunt Ruby.

Reluctantly, Henry followed his ᵤsin up the wide staircase.

216

"I bet you're scared of the dark," said Steve.

"'Course I'm not," said Henry.

"That's good," said Steve. "This is my room," he added, opening the door to an enormous bedroom. Horrid Henry stared longingly at the shelves filled to bursting with zillions of toys and games.

"Of course all *my* toys are brand new. Don't you dare touch anything," hissed Steve. "They're all mine and only *I* can play with them."

Henry scowled. When he was king he'd use Steve's head for target practice.

They continued all the way to the top. Goodness, this old house was big, thought Henry.

Steve opened the door to a large attic bedroom, with brand new pink and blue flowered wallpaper, a four-poster bed, an enormous polished wood wardrobe, and two large windows.

"You're in the haunted room," said Steve casually.

"Great!" said Henry. "I love ghosts." It would take more than a silly ghost to frighten *him*.

"Don't believe me if you don't want to," said Steve. "Just don't blame me when the ghost starts wailing."

"You're nothing but a big fat liar," said Henry. He was sure Steve was lying. He was absolutely sure Steve was lying.

He was one million percent sure that
Steve was lying.

He's just trying to pay me back for
Christmas, thought Henry.

Steve shrugged. "Suit yourself. See that
stain on the carpet?"

Henry looked down at something
brownish.

"That's where the ghost vaporized,"
whispered Steve. "Of course if you're too
scared to sleep here ..."

Henry would rather have walked on
hot coals than admit being scared to
Steve.

He yawned, as if he'd never heard
anything so boring.

"I'm looking forward to meeting the
ghost," said Henry.

"Good," said Steve.

"Supper, boys!" called Aunt Ruby.

Henry lay in bed. Somehow he'd
survived the dreadful meal and Stuck-Up
Steve's bragging about his expensive
clothes, toys and trainers. Now here he
was, alone in the attic at the top of the
house. He'd jumped into bed, carefully
avoiding the faded brown patch on the
floor. He was sure it was just spilled cola
or something, but just in case . . .

Henry looked around him. The only thing he didn't like was the huge wardrobe opposite the bed. It loomed up in the darkness at him. You could hide a body in that wardrobe, thought Henry, then rather wished he hadn't.

"Oooooooooh."

Henry stiffened.

Had he just imagined the sound of someone moaning?

Silence.

Nothing, thought Henry, snuggling down under the covers. Just the wind.

"Ooooooooooh."

This time the moaning was a fraction louder. The hairs on Henry's neck stood up. He gripped the sheets tightly.

"Haaaaaahhhhhhh."

Henry sat up.

"Haaaaaaaaahhhhhhhhhhhh."

The ghostly breathy moaning sound was not coming from outside. It appeared to be coming from inside the giant wardrobe.

Quickly, Henry switched on the bed-side light.

What am I going to do? thought Henry. He wanted to run screaming to his aunt.

But the truth was, Henry was too frightened to move.

Some dreadful moaning thing was inside the wardrobe.

Just waiting to get *him*.

And then Horrid Henry remembered who he was. Leader of a pirate gang. Afraid of nothing (except injections).

I'll just get up and check inside that wardrobe, he thought. Am I a man or a mouse?

Mouse! he thought.

He did not move.

"Oooooooooaaaaahhhhhh," moaned

the THING. The unearthly noises were getting louder.

Shall I wait here for IT to get me, or shall I make a move first? thought Henry. Silently, he reached under the bed for his Goo-Shooter.

Then slowly, he swung his feet over the bed. Tiptoe. Tiptoe. Tiptoe.

Holding his breath, Horrid Henry stood outside the wardrobe.

"HAHAHAHAHAHAHAHAHHA!"

Henry jumped. Then he flung open the door and fired.

SPLAT!

"HAHAHAHAHAHAHAHAHAH AHAHAughhhhhhh –"

The wardrobe was empty.

Except for something small and greeny-black on the top shelf.

It looked like – it was!

Henry reached up and took it.

It was a cassette player. Covered in green goo.

Inside was a tape. It was called "Dr Jekyll's Spooky Sounds."

Steve, thought Horrid Henry grimly. REVENGE!

"Did you sleep well, dear?" asked Aunt Ruby at breakfast.

"Like a log," said Henry.

"No strange noises?" asked Steve.

"No," smiled Henry sweetly. "Why, did you hear something?"

Steve looked disappointed. Horrid Henry kept his face blank. He couldn't wait for the evening.

Horrid Henry spent a busy day.
He went ice-skating.
He went to the cinema.
He played football.

After supper, Henry went straight to bed.

"It's been a lovely day," he said. "But I'm tired. Goodnight, Aunt Ruby. Goodnight, Steve."

"Goodnight, Henry," said Ruby.

Steve ignored him.

But Henry did not go to his bedroom. Instead he sneaked into Steve's.

He wriggled under Steve's bed and lay there, waiting.

Soon Steve came into the room. Henry resisted the urge to reach out and seize Steve's skinny leg. He had something much scarier in mind.

He heard Steve putting on his blue bunny pyjamas and jumping into bed. Henry waited until the room was dark.

Steve lay above him, humming to himself.

"Dooby dooby dooby do," sang Steve.

Slowly, Henry reached up, and ever so slightly, poked the mattress.

Silence.

"Dooby dooby dooby do," sang Steve,
a little more quietly.

Henry reached up and poked the
mattress again.

Steve sat up.

Then he lay back.

Henry poked the mattress again, ever
so slightly.

"Must be my imagination," muttered
Steve.

Henry allowed several moments to
pass. Then he twitched the duvet.

"Mummy," whimpered Steve.

Jab! Henry gave the mattress a definite
poke.

"AHHHHHHHHHHHH!"
screamed Steve. He leaped up and ran
out of the room. "MUMMY! HELP!
MONSTERS!"

Henry scrambled out of the room
and ran silently up to his attic. Quick
as he could he put on his pyjamas, then
clattered noisily back down the stairs
to Steve's.

Aunt Ruby was on her hands and
knees, peering under the bed. Steve
was shivering and quivering in the
corner.

"There's nothing here, Steve," she said
firmly.

"What's wrong?" asked Henry.

"Nothing," muttered Steve.

"You're not *scared* of the dark, are you?"
said Henry.

"Back to bed, boys," said Aunt Ruby.
She left the room.

"Ahhhhh, Mummy, help! Monsters!"
mimicked Henry, sticking out his
tongue.

"MUM!" wailed Steve. "Henry's being
horrid!"

"GO TO BED, BOTH OF YOU!" shrieked Ruby.

"Watch out for monsters," said Henry.

Steve did not move from his corner.

"Want to swap rooms tonight?" said Henry.

Steve did not wait to be asked twice.

"Oh yes," said Steve.

"Go on up," said Henry. "Sweet dreams."

Steve dashed out of his bedroom as fast as he could.

Tee hee, thought Horrid Henry, pulling Steve's toys down from the shelves. Now, what would he play with first?

Oh, yes. He'd left a few spooky sounds of his own under the attic bed – just in case.

3

HORRID HENRY'S
SCHOOL FAIR

"Henry! Peter! I need your donations to the school fair NOW!"

Mum was in a bad mood. She was helping Moody Margaret's mum organize the fair and had been nagging Henry for ages to give away some of his old games and toys. Horrid Henry hated giving. He liked getting.

Horrid Henry stood in his bedroom. Everything he owned was on the floor.

"How about giving away those bricks?" said Mum. "You never play with them any more."

"NO!" said Henry. They were bound

to come in useful some day.

"How about some soft toys? When was the last time you played with Spotty Dog?"

"NO!" said Horrid Henry. "He's mine!"

Perfect Peter appeared in the doorway dragging two enormous sacks.

"Here's my contribution to the school fair, Mum," said Perfect Peter.

Mum peeped inside the bags.

"Are you sure you want to give away so many toys?" said Mum.

"Yes," said Peter. "I'd like other children to have fun playing with them."

"What a generous boy you are, Peter," she said, giving him a big hug.

Henry scowled. Peter could give away all his toys, for all Henry cared. Henry wanted to keep everything.

Wait! How could he have forgotten?

Henry reached under his bed and pulled out a large box hidden under a blanket. The box contained all the useless, horrible presents Henry had ever received. Packs of hankies. Vests with ducks on them. A nature guide. Uggh! Henry hated nature. Why would anyone want to waste their time looking at pictures of flowers and trees?

And then, right at the bottom, was the worst present of all. A Walkie-Talkie-

Burpy-Slurpy-Teasy-Weasy Doll. He'd got it for Christmas from a great-aunt he'd never met. The card she'd written was still attached.

Dear Henrietta

I thought this doll would be perfect for a sweet little two-year-old like you! Take good care of your new baby!

Love

Great-Aunt Greta

Even worse, she'd sent Peter something brilliant.

Dear Pete
You must be a teenager by now and too old for toys, so here's £25. Don't spend it all on sweets!
Love
Great-Aunt Greta

Henry had screamed and begged, but Peter got to keep the money, and Henry was stuck with the doll. He was far too embarrassed to try to sell it, so the doll just lived hidden under his bed with all the other rotten gifts.

"Take that," said Henry, giving the doll a kick.

"Mama Mama Mama!" burbled the doll. "Baby burp!"

237

"Not Great-Aunt Greta's present!" said Mum.

"Take it or leave it," said Henry. "You can have the rest as well."

Mum sighed. "Some lucky children are going to be very happy." She took the hateful presents and put them in the jumble sack.

Phew! He'd got rid of that doll at last! He'd lived in terror of Rude Ralph or Moody Margaret coming over and finding it. Now he'd never have to see that burping slurping long-haired thing again.

Henry crept into the spare room where Mum was keeping all the donated toys and games for the fair. Henry thought he'd have a quick poke around and see what good stuff would be for sale tomorrow. That way he could make a dash and be first in the queue.

There were rolls of raffle tickets, bottles of wine, the barrel for the lucky dip, and sacks and sacks of toys. Wow, what a hoard! Henry just had to move that rolled up poster out of the way and start rummaging!

Henry pushed aside the poster and then stopped.

I wonder what this is, he thought. I think I'll just unroll it and have a little peek. No harm in that.

Carefully, he untied the ribbon and laid the poster flat on the floor. Then he gasped.

This wasn't jumble. It was the Treasure Map! Whoever guessed where the treasure was hidden always won a fabulous prize. Last year Sour Susan had won a skateboard. The year before Jolly Josh had won a Super Soaker 2000. Boy it sure was worth trying to find that treasure! Horrid Henry usually had at least five goes. But his luck was so bad he had never even come close.

Henry looked at the map. There was the island, with its caves and lagoons, and the sea surrounding it, filled with whales

and sharks and pirate ships. The map
was divided into a hundred numbered
squares. Somewhere under one of those
squares was an X.

I'll just admire the lovely picture,
thought Henry. He stared and stared.
No X. He ran his hands over the map.
No X.

Henry sighed. It was so unfair!
He never won anything. And this year
the prize was sure to be a Super Soaker
5000.

Henry lifted the map to roll it up.
As he raised the thick paper to the light,
a large, unmistakable X was suddenly
visible beneath square 42.

The treasure was just under the whale's eye.

He had discovered the secret.

"YES!" said Horrid Henry, punching the air. "It's my lucky day, at last!"

But wait. Mum was in charge of the Treasure Map stall. If he was first in the queue and instantly bagged square 42 she was sure to be suspicious. So how could he let a few other children go first, but make sure none of them chose the right square? And then suddenly, he had a brilliant, spectacular idea . . .

"Tra la la la la!" trilled Horrid Henry, as he, Peter, Mum and Dad walked to the school fair.

"You're cheerful today, Henry," said Dad.

"I'm feeling lucky," said Horrid Henry.

He burst into the playground and went straight to the Treasure Map stall. A large queue of eager children keen to pay 20p for a chance to guess had already formed. There was the mystery prize, a large, tempting, Super Soaker-sized box. Wheeee!

Rude Ralph was first in line.

"Psst, Ralph," whispered Henry. "I know where X marks the spot. I'll tell you if you give me 50p."

"Deal," said Ralph.

"92," whispered Henry.

"Thanks!" said Ralph. He wrote his name in square 92 and walked off, whistling.

Moody Margaret was next.

"Pssst, Margaret," whispered Henry. "I know where X marks the spot."

"Where?" said Margaret.

"Pay me 50p and I'll tell you," whispered Henry.

"Why should I trust you?" said Margaret loudly.

Henry shrugged.

"Don't trust me then, and I'll tell Susan," said Henry.

Margaret gave Henry 50p.

"2," whispered Horrid Henry.

Margaret wrote her name in square 2, and skipped off.

Henry told Lazy Linda the treasure square was 4.

Henry told Dizzy Dave the treasure square was 100.

Weepy William was told 22.

Anxious Andrew was told 14.

Then Henry thought it was time he bagged the winning square. He made sure none of the children he'd tricked were nearby, then pushed into the queue behind Beefy Bert. His pockets bulged with cash.

"What number do you want, Bert?" asked Henry's mum.

"I dunno," said Bert.

"Hi Mum," said Henry. "Here's my 20p. Hmmm, now where could that treasure be?"

Horrid Henry pretended to study the map.

"I think I'll try 37," he said. "No wait, 84. Wait, wait, I'm still deciding . . ."

"Hurry up Henry," said Mum. "Other children want to have a go."

"Okay, 42," said Henry.

Mum looked at him. Henry smiled at her and wrote his name in the square.

Then he sauntered off.

He could feel that Super Soaker in his hands already. Wouldn't it be fun to spray the teachers!

Horrid Henry had a fabulous day. He threw wet sponges at Miss Battle-Axe in the "Biff a Teacher" stall. He joined in his class square dance. He got a marble in the lucky dip. Henry didn't even scream when Perfect Peter won a box of notelets in the raffle and Henry didn't win anything, despite spending £3 on tickets.

"TIME TO FIND THE WINNER
OF THE TREASURE MAP
COMPETITION," boomed a
voice over the playground. Everyone
stampeded to the stall.

Suddenly Henry had a terrible
thought. What if Mum had switched the
X to a different spot at the last minute?
He couldn't bear it. He absolutely

couldn't bear it. He had to have that Super Soaker!

"And the winning number is . . ." Mum lifted up the Treasure Map . . . "42! The winner is – Henry."

"Yes!" screamed Henry.

"What?" screamed Rude Ralph, Moody Margaret, Lazy Linda, Weepy William, and Anxious Andrew.

"Here's your prize, Henry," said Mum.

She handed Henry the enormous box.

"Congratulations." She did not look very pleased.

Eagerly, Henry tore off the wrapping paper. His prize was a Walkie-Talkie-Burpy-Slurpy-Teasy-Weasy Doll.

"Mama Mama Mama!" burbled the doll. "Baby Slurp!"

"AAARRGGGHHHH!" howled Henry.

4

HORRID HENRY
MINDS HIS MANNERS

"Henry and Peter! You've got mail!" said Mum.

Henry and Peter thundered down the stairs. Horrid Henry snatched his letter and tore open the green envelope. The foul stink of mouldy socks wafted out.

Yo Henry!

Marvin the Maniac here. You sound just like the kind of crazy guy we want on Gross-Out! Be at TV Centre next Saturday at 9.00 a.m. and gross us out! It's a live broadcast, so anything can happen!

Marvin

"I've been invited to be a contestant on *Gross-Out!*" screamed Henry, dancing up and down the stairs. It was a dream come true. "I'll be shooting it out with Tank Thomas and Tapioca Tina while eating as much ice cream as I can!"

"Absolutely not!" said Mum. "You will not go on that disgusting show!"

"Agreed," said Dad. "That show is revolting."

"It's meant to be revolting!" said Horrid Henry. "That's the point."

"N-O spells no," said Mum.

"You're the meanest, most horrible

252

parents in the whole world," screamed
Henry. "I hate you!" He threw himself
on the sofa and wailed. "I WANT TO
BE ON *GROSS-OUT*! I WANT
TO BE ON *GROSS-OUT*!"

Perfect Peter opened his letter. The
sweet smell of lavender wafted out.

Dear Peter,
    What a wonderful letter you wrote
on the importance of perfect manners!
As a reward I would like to invite
you to be my special guest on the live
broadcast of Manners With Maggie

next Saturday at TV Centre
at 9:00 a.m.

You will be showing the girls and boys
at home how to fold a hankie perfectly,
how to hold a knife and fork elegantly,
and how to eat spaghetti beautifully with
a fork and spoon.

I am very much looking forward to
meeting you and to enjoying your lovely
manners in person.

Sincerely,
Maggie.

"I've been invited to appear on *Manners With Maggie!*" said Peter, beaming.

"That's wonderful, Peter!" said Mum. She hugged him.

"I'm so proud of you," said Dad. He hugged him.

Horrid Henry stopped screaming.

"That's not fair!" said Henry. "If Peter

can be on his favourite TV show why can't I be on mine?"

Mum and Dad looked at each other.

"I suppose he does have a point," said Dad. He sighed.

"And we don't have to tell anyone he's on," said Mum. She sighed.

"All right, Henry. You can be a contestant."

"YIPPEE!" squealed Henry, stomping on the sofa and doing his victory jig. "I'm going to be a star! *Gross-Out* here I come!"

The great day arrived at last. Horrid Henry had been practising so hard with his Goo-Shooter he could hit Perfect Peter's nose at thirty paces. He'd also been practising shovelling ice cream into his mouth as fast as he could, until Mum caught him.

255

Perfect Peter had been practising so hard folding his hankie that he could do it with one hand. And no one could twirl spaghetti with a spoon as beautifully or hold a knife and fork as elegantly as Perfect Peter.

At nine a.m. sharp, Mum, Henry, and Peter walked into TV Centre. Henry was starving. He'd skipped breakfast, to have more room for all the ice cream he'd be gobbling.

Horrid Henry wore old jeans and dirty trainers. Perfect Peter wore a jacket and tie.

A woman with red hair and freckles rushed up to them with a clipboard.

"Hi, I'm Super Sally. Welcome to TV Centre. I'm sorry boys, we'll have to dash, we're running late. Come with me to the guests' waiting room. You're both on in five minutes."

"Can't I stay with them?" said Mum.

"Parents to remain downstairs in the parents' room," said Super Sally sternly. "You can watch on the monitors there."

"Good luck, boys," said Mum, waving.

Sally stared at Peter as they hurried down the hall.

"Aren't you worried about getting those smart clothes dirty?" said Sally.

Peter looked shocked.

"I *never* get my clothes dirty," he said.

"There's always a first time," chortled Sally. "Here's the waiting room. Studios one and two where you'll be filming are through those doors at the end."

In the room was a sofa and two tables. One, marked *Gross-Out*, was groaning with sweets, crisps and fizzy drinks.

The second, labelled *Manners with Maggie*, was laid with a crisp white cloth. A few dainty vegetables were displayed on a china plate.

Horrid Henry suddenly felt nervous. Today was his day to be a TV star! Had he practised enough? And he was so hungry! His stomach tightened.

"I need a wee," said Horrid Henry.

"Toilets next door," said Super Sally. "Be quick. You're on in one minute."

Perfect Peter didn't feel in the least nervous. Practice made perfect, and he knew he was. What disgusting food, he thought, wandering over to the *Gross-Out* table.

A man wearing combat fatigues dashed into the room.

"Ah, there you are!" he boomed. "Come along! It's your big moment!"

"I'm ready," said Peter, waving his handkerchief.

The man pushed him through the
door marked Stage 1.

Henry returned.

A lady in high heels and a pearl
necklace poked her head round the door.

"You're on, dear!" said the lady.
"Goodness, you look a little untidy.
Never mind, can't be helped." And she
ushered Henry through the door marked
Stage 2.

Henry found himself on a brightly
lit stage. He blinked in the brilliant lights.

"Let's give a warm welcome to today's
guest!" cried a voice. A *female* voice.

The studio audience exploded into
applause.

Henry froze. Who was that woman?

Where was Marvin the Maniac?

Something's wrong, he thought. This
was not the set of *Gross-Out*. It was a
pink and yellow kitchen. Yet it looked
vaguely familiar . . .

Meanwhile, on Stage 1, Perfect Peter shrank back in horror as two gigantic children carrying Goo-Shooters and massive bowls of ice cream advanced towards him. A presenter, laughing like a hyena, egged them on.

"You're not Maggie!" said Peter. "And I don't know how to use a —"

"Get him guys!" squealed Marvin the Maniac.

"HELLLLP!" shrieked Peter.

SPLAT!

Back on Stage 2, Henry suddenly
realized where he was.

"Now don't be shy, darling!" said the
presenter, walking quickly to Henry and
taking him firmly by the hand. "Peter's
here to show us how to fold a hankie
and how to eat beautifully!" It was
Maggie. From *Manners with Maggie*.

What could Henry do? He was
on live TV! There were the cameras

zooming in on him. If he screamed
there'd been a terrible mistake that
would ruin the show. And hadn't he
heard that the show must go on? Even a
dreadful show like *Manners with Maggie*?

Henry strolled onto centre stage,
smiling and bowing.

"Now Peter will show us the perfect
way to fold a hankie."

Horrid Henry felt a sneeze coming.

"AAAACHOOO!" he sneezed. Then
he wiped his nose on his sleeve.

The audience giggled. Maggie looked
stunned.

"The ... hankie," she prompted.

"Oh yeah," said Henry, feeling in his pockets. He removed a few crumpled wads of ancient tissue.

"Here, use mine," said Maggie smoothly.

Henry took the beautifully embroidered square of silky cloth and scrunched it into a ball. Then he stuffed it into his pocket.

"Nothing to it," said Henry. "Scrunch and stuff. But why bother with a hankie when a sleeve works so much better?"

Maggie gulped. "Very funny, Peter dear! *We* know he's only joking, don't we, children! Now we'll show the girls and boys –"

But Horrid Henry had noticed the table, set with a chocolate cake and a large bowl of spaghetti. Yummy! And Henry hadn't eaten anything for ages.

"Hey, that cake looks great!" inter-

rupted Henry. He dashed to the table,
dug out a nice big hunk and shoved it
in his mouth.

"Stop eating!" hissed Maggie. "We
haven't finished the hankie demonstra-
tion yet!"

But Henry didn't stop.

"Yummy," he said, licking his fingers.

Maggie looked like she was going to
faint.

"Show the girls and boys how to use
a knife and fork elegantly, Peter," she
said, with gritted teeth.

"Nah, a knife and fork slows you

down too much. I *always* eat with my fingers. See?"

Horrid Henry waved his chocolate-covered hands.

"I'm sure it was just the excitement of being on TV that made you forget to offer *me* a slice of cake," prompted Maggie. She gazed in horror at the cake, now with a gaping hole on the side.

"But I want to eat it all myself!" said Horrid Henry. "I'm starving! Get your own cake."

"Now I'm going to teach you the proper way to eat spaghetti," said Maggie stiffly, pretending she hadn't heard. "Which we should have done first, of course, as we do not eat dessert before the main course."

"I do!" said Henry.

"Hold your spoon in your left hand, fork in your right, pick up a teensy tiny amount of spaghetti and twirl twirl twirl.

Let's see if my little helper can do it.
I'm sure he's been practising at home."

" 'Course," lied Henry. How hard
could it be to twirl spaghetti? Henry
picked up his spoon, plunged his fork
into an enormous pile of spaghetti and
started to twirl. The spaghetti flew round
the kitchen. A few strands landed on
Maggie's head.

"Whoops," said Henry. "I'll try again."
Before Maggie could stop him he'd
seized another huge forkful.

"It keeps falling off," said Henry.
"Listen, kids, use your fingers — it's
faster." Then Henry scooped a handful
of spaghetti and crammed it into his
mouth.

"It's good," mumbled Henry, chewing
loudly with his mouth open.

"Stop! Stop!" said Maggie. Her voice
rose to a polite scream.

"What's wrong?" said Henry, trailing
great strings of spaghetti out of his
mouth.

Suddenly Henry heard a high-
pitched howl. Then Perfect Peter burst
onto the set, covered in green goo,
followed by whooping children waving
Goo-Shooters.

"Maggie! Save me!" shrieked Peter,
dropping his shooter and hurling himself

268

into her arms. "They're trying to make me eat between meals!"

"Get away from me, you horrible child!" screamed Maggie.

It was the Goo-Shooter gang at last! Better late than never, thought Henry.

"Yeee haaa!" Henry snatched Peter's Goo-Shooter, jumped onto the table and sprayed Tapioca Tina, Tank Thomas and most of the audience. Gleefully, they returned fire. Henry took a step back, and stepped into the spaghetti.

SPLAT!

"Help!" screamed Maggie, green goo and spaghetti dripping from her face.

"Help!" screamed Peter, green goo and spaghetti dripping from his hair.

"CUT!" shouted the director.

Horrid Henry was lying on the comfy black chair flicking channels. Sadly, *Manners with Maggie* was no longer on TV since Maggie had been dragged screaming off the set. *Mischief with Mildred* would be on soon. Henry thought he'd give it a try.

HORRID HENRY
AND THE SECRET CLUB

Horrid Henry gets an injection,
torments his little brother Perfect Peter,
creates havoc at his own birthday party,
and plans sweet revenge when
Moody Margaret won't let him
into her Secret Club.

HORRID HENRY
TRICKS THE TOOTH FAIRY

Horrid Henry tries to trick the
Tooth Fairy, has Moody Margaret
to stay and sends her packing, makes
teachers run screaming from school,
and single-handedly wrecks a wedding.